Rock Slide

Rock Slide

Book Seven of
the Clint Mason Series

by

William F. Martin

authorHOUSE®

AuthorHouse™
1663 Liberty Drive
Bloomington, IN 47403
www.authorhouse.com
Phone: 1-800-839-8640

Published by AuthorHouse   11/06/2014

ISBN: 978-1-4969-5215-8 (sc)
ISBN: 978-1-4969-5216-5 (e)

Contents

Chapter 1

The dust was still boiling out of the gorge just south of Silverton. Half a dozen heavily armed riders were looking down the raw cut of the steep mountain. With their rifles pointing down the slope, the eyes of all the riders were searching the rubble for any signs of life. The smell of dynamite smoke was still in the air.

A rider far to the left let out a shout as he pointed to an object far down the rock slide. One of the other riders on a big black stallion pulled out some field glasses and scanned the area of interest. He spotted the mangled corpse of a dead horse among the big boulders. The field glasses were passed around the group. It was the consensus of all these riders that the dead horse belonged to the man they had been trying to kill and rob.

Two riders dismounted and started the dangerous climb down the rocks to the dead horse. The boulders were loose from the dynamite charges, and several small rock slides resulted as the men slowly made their way to the horse. Their goal was to confirm that its rider was dead, and recover a large cache of gold coins and bars. A hat was found near the dead horse. With considerable effort, the two men were able to pull the saddlebags laden with gold from the half-buried dead horse. One good repeater rifle was also retrieved. The only sign of the downed rider was his fancy flat-crown hat, black with silver trim and wide brim. The heavy saddlebags and black hat were hauled back up the dangerous rock slide face to the waiting riders.

There was considerable discussion among the six riders. Eventually, the big man on the black stallion pointed out some instructions. Three riders headed north back toward Silverton. One of these three had the fancy black hat. He threw his old hat into the air with two of the riders shooting at it. He then put the black hat with all the silver trim squarely on his own head. Those three riders then disappeared around a big curve in the high mountainous road toward Silverton.

The apparent leader of the band, the tall man with field glasses riding the black stallion, continued to scan the boulders below looking for any sign of movement or life. The sun was just dropping below the mountain ridge to the west when the remaining riders, the gold-laden saddlebags, and the repeating rifle finally headed south toward Durango.

As the sun rays left the rocks, the cool breeze that had been moving up the canyon turned to bitter cold. The darkness came on fast as heavy clouds moved along with the cold wind. The dynamite smoke and dust were quickly replaced with crisp cold mountain air.

Clint Mason pulled himself erect out of the dusty hole he had dived into. The giant tree stump and rock pit had saved his life. The first stick of dynamite had only put up dust, but the sound and pressure spooked his horse. By pure reflex he had abandoned his saddle and horse just before it went over the cliff. The huge dust cloud from the first explosion obscured his dismount. The second much larger blast occurred just as his horse went over the edge. That second blast took out a big section of the road shoulder. The rock slide that followed shook the giant tree stump where Clint had taken shelter. He was expecting the mountain to give way at any moment. Looking below, the dust cloud was too dense to see where his horse had landed, so he just buried himself into the hole on the downhill side of the stump. The rain of the dust and rock came down on him like a giant hail storm. He took a few hard hits, but with no permanent damage. His self-control took charge and he lay perfectly still for over two hours. The pitch black of a cloudy night had set in when he finally crawled out of his dusty rock tomb.

He had lost his hat, bed roll, horse, saddlebags and all his supplies. The only thing he had left was his life, one side gun and a money belt. The ringing in his ears was gradually lessening, but his orientation as to exactly where he was and what to do next was slow to take form in his head.

The first instinct was to run, but where? He had no idea about the people that had ambushed him with sticks of dynamite. They had killed his horse and probably stolen his major gold cache. If he was to avenge this attack, the identity of those responsible must be determined. His sharp brain started to engage.

The best count of horses was six as his memory searched through the past incident. He was not sure his ears were working as well as usual. The tracks on the mountain trail with their new fine mist of rock dust would tell the tale. He would need to read the tracks before anyone else passed this point. It was too dark to see now unless the clouds parted to let moonlight shine over the fresh tracks.

A major concern was to leave no trace of his survival. The most important element was his life. The cold wind and his dust-filled injuries were driving a death chill into his bones.

Some small brush branches lay near him. These sticks and dried leaves served as a broom as he crawled up the steep bank to the road bed.

Stirring up the dusty trail behind him was easy with the rock dust that covered everything in the area. A few breaks in the cloud cover gradually let the moonlight show Clint the hoof prints. His memory was so good that he soon had the images of the horses that had last stood on this trail. When time, paper and pen became available, he would be able to draw each hoof set in extreme detail.

Shelter was the next pressing need, then water and food. He moved across the road and up the steep slope until he found some low-lying evergreens. The branch broom was in constant motion covering his tracks until he found safety under a sprawling evergreen. The pine needles were thick and the tree branches hung close to the ground. It took only a few minutes to burrow into the needle bed and pull the low hanging branches down. The climb up the steep slope had generated some heat in his body that he tried to retain.

The bed of needles and leaves proved to be a well-insulated nest. Curling into a tight circle, his body heat was conserved and he fell asleep.

The dripping rain water quickly brought his mind to full alert. He was not wet yet, but the steady rain on his nest would soon begin to seep through. The morning light was just beginning to bring the earth into focus. The wind had settled down a little, but the chill was still in his bones. The rock cuts in his arms, legs and back were demanding his attention. He examined each cut he could reach to see if any serious damage had been done to muscles or tendons. The loss of blood had been minimal. Even though he ached all over and was joint stiff, the blasts had not done any major damage except to his pride. The ringing in his ears had finally stopped and his excellent sight was restored.

His location was about midway between Silverton and Durango. This rough road was familiar to Clint as he had traveled between the two towns many times. He recalled that there were several abandoned miner's cabins along the river below. A few of the old structures were up along this high road where teamsters would stop overnight as they hauled supplies from Durango up to the mining camps. A shelter of any kind would be helpful until he was in better shape to travel. He needed a horse and some pen and paper to draw the hoof prints before the images grew dim. His hat had gone north to Silverton with three of the riders. This would be his first target for revenge that he would be able to identify. Thinking of his black, flat-crown hat, he remembered that the robber that took it had thrown his own into the air for target practice. A hat was a valuable item when the cold air blew or the hot sun bore down on a man. It took Clint only a few minutes to find the target hat. A smile came over his sore face when it turned out the hat had no bullet holes. At least two of the bandits were not that good with their pistols.

No traffic had come along the Durango to Silverton trail since his ambush late yesterday. He took his time examining the trail, but the rain had covered the hoof prints. He would have to make do with the moonlight prints he had seen last evening. He did not venture down the steep boulder rock face to his dead horse. His energy was needed to find better shelter and a new horse. There was plenty of money in his waistband. Reserve poker money was something he always kept close at hand. This cache of gold coins was more than most western cowboys made in a year's time even though it was a small fraction in value compared to the heavy saddlebags the robbers had taken. The loss of this money made Clint mad, but the killing of his fantastic stallion bubbled up the deep need for justice and revenge.

Patience and intelligence were the words that Clint kept whispering to himself. He knew that he could be ruthless. His history was filled with killings, but Clint could justify each one to himself. He even scolded himself for bringing this ambush down on his head. He had played poker in Silverton without patience or intelligence, openly winning large sums. Then he had carelessly set out on the main road to Durango without any of his normal clever precautions. He loved gambling and the high emotions that flowed over him following the large poker winnings. He had thrown caution to the winds and had almost lost his life as well. Feeling the cuts and bruises on his arms, legs, and back reinforced the need for brains over impulse. Revenge he would seek, but on his terms. There would be no justice until all six gutless roadside thieves were made to pay for killing his horse. Getting his money back would be a bonus, but the real goal was to have all six riders pay with his own pound of flesh... each and every last one of them.

Chapter 2

It was midday before Clint approached the first abandoned cabin on the high road. The sun was bearing down on his sore back. Several of the cuts had opened up a little, but were no real threat to his survival. The pain only cemented his desire for action. The cabin was empty, but was clearly often used. Clint found some paper and a pencil. The next two hours were spent drawing each hoof print and organizing them into sets. Clint had known for some years that his mind was sharper than the average. His ability to recall the exact details of each hoof print impressed him. This memory explained why his poker skills were second to none. Those stolen bags of gold had been won through his remarkable gambling skills.

A thorough rummaging through the cabin did yield some iodine and cloth to treat his wounds. Also some rope and a bridle were found. These would be useful if he could find a stray horse. A fresh spring near the cabin helped quench his thirst. The afternoon sun was still hot so Clint sought out a safe bed under a big spruce tree some 50 yards from the cabin. The sun angle indicated late afternoon when noise up the trail broke the peace and calm of his afternoon nap.

Three heavily loaded wagons with six horses each pulled off the road at the old cabin. There were at least nine men in the group, both drivers and guards. The layover lasted about two hours. With canteens full of fresh water and a cold lunch in their bellies, the three wagons pulled on through toward Silverton. Knowing this traffic around the cabin and on the road would cover his tracks, he headed up the road well behind the wagons. Traveling on the road was much faster than his earlier trip from the ambush site to that first cabin. Until now, he had kept off the roadway most of the time to leave no trace that someone had survived that landslide and dynamite blasts.

The steep climb toward Silverton was really slowing the freight wagons. Clint had to be careful not to close the distance between them. The sound of steel wheels against a hard rock roadbed sent a signal to Clint, and a careful peek around the bend located the wagons being stopped at some old buildings with a corral. The teamsters were changing teams for fresh ones. This must be a way station where the freighters keep extra horses for the hard climb into Silverton. They probably change the horses back on the return trip to Durango. This way station had seven wagons parked along a low shed and corral. The main cabin had plenty of smoke spewing out its chimney. Clint could smell the bacon cooking and see it cooking on a big iron skillet. His stomach was begging for food, but he settled in for a long wait.

The Durango to Silverton high road hugged the mountain hundreds of feet above the rushing waters of the river below. The views from some of the curves of the mountain road were breathtaking. The mountain peaks pierced the landscape as they extended above the tree line. Sometimes he thought that the gold and silver hidden in these beautiful mountains brought out a dark side of mankind. The greed to get rich quickly without labor drew a type of people that could lead to trouble.

The trouble really started when the gold seekers ran head-on into the realization that mining was dirty, hard labor. That was the decision point. They could settle into a hard life of hard rock mining. Many just gave up and went on west or back east to civilization. But, some chose the life of living off another's sweat through corruption, thievery and gambling. Clint had to recognize that he had chosen the gambling option. His choice had made him rich more than once, but it almost cost him his life time and time again. He loved the poker games and the challenges between men. The gambling tables had always rewarded his exceptional skills with math, memory and reading people. The gun skills that had come natural to him as a young man had helped to keep him alive so far. The aches and pains of his current condition reminded him that he was not infallible. A quick reflex had aided his escape from the roadside blast but it had been mostly luck. A good survival plan does not depend on luck. He had to be a little smarter and more cautious than his last gambling run in Silverton. The finger of blame pointed at him. There would always be people ready to separate a person from his hard-earned livelihood.

The challenge to the individual is recognizing reality and then navigating a life that is rewarding but not restrictive due to the evil that does exist. Bad things do happen to good people, but that fact should not limit their seeking for a happier time. The journey should be as enjoyable as the prizes we seek. If the journey gets cut short, it's better to have lived well.

The sun had set and the night chill had moved into Clint's hiding place well above the way station. Two more wagons had joined the group. It did appear that the freighters were settling in for the night. There were more than 20 men milling around one of the buildings where the good smelling smoke was rising. Even at this distance Clint could tell that many of the men did not know each other and that they were drinking heavily. His rumbling stomach finally overrode his caution, so a slow move was made toward the smell of food. A stop at the stables yielded an old jacket to cover his fancy gambling shirt that was clearly spotted with his own blood.

The log cabin's central room was jammed with drinkers, eaters and poker players. He slipped unnoticed to a stool along the bar. The rough looking bartender took his order for beer, steak and potatoes without a glance into his face. Spring water would have been better, but the beer was a good second. It only took minutes for a big beef steak with ample skillet fried potatoes to be slid before him. One good part of really being hungry is that food tastes heavenly. Clint paced himself so he could take in the whole room as he ate. He sipped the beer and slowly ate the meal, savoring every bite.

It soon became evident that the bunkhouse was a self-serve arrangement. A big stack of blankets and towels were stacked next to the door that led to the bunkhouse. An elderly Chinese man collected the coins and handed out the blankets, towels and a number for the bed. In due time, Clint drifted over to the Chinaman, paid the fee, and collected his bed number and blanket. The bunkhouse was not too bad. It looked like a stable with stalls and small cots. The noise level was constant, but the walls between each bed did provide some relief. A large bulk of a man moved up and down the long aisle to remove anyone that was causing too much noise or staggering drunk.

A steady rain on the metal roof reminded Clint he had made a good choice. Sleep came sooner than he expected but it felt good. The dim light of dawn was accented with people moving and getting ready for the road. Rummaging through a box full of leftover clothes yielded some useful items. The rags were put on and his good clothes were rolled up. His good gambling clothes had some of his blood on them plus a few holes from the rock blast. The quality of his own clothes would also stand out. Clint understood that, to survive, he must blend in without any suspicion of his true identity.

A thorough sweep of the hitching rails did not provide any hoof prints that matched those from the rock slide bandits. The ground was compressed and muddy from last night's rain. If there had been tracks from the horses he was trying to find, they were completely washed away. The wind was drying the ground rapidly. In a few hours it would be a good time to search the trail leading out of the way station. His best guess was that those three riders had made it back to Silverton before last night. He had spent a complete day of walking and keeping off the trail.

Patience was the word that Clint kept repeating to himself. In due time he would extract his revenge on all six bandits that had killed his fine horse, stolen his gold and took his hat.

There was a big ruckus down by the stables where the teamsters were preparing to move out. A big circle of men had formed where all were shouting and laughing. Clint moved closer cautiously to see what all the fuss was about. It turned out that four men were fighting just outside the big double stable doors. The area was six inches deep in mud and manure. It looked like the two sets of teamsters were beating each other into raw meat. There did not seem to be any blood, but all four men were covered with black mud from head to toe. The ground was so slippery that the fighters could not get a good foothold. It was a comedy show. The crowd of hard working men was enjoying the fight.

One big fellow put a real haymaker blow upside another's head. The struck man staggered and fell back against the watering trough. The big man that had delivered the knock-down blow turned to help his buddy against the third man. The downed man shook his head to clear the cobwebs. His hand found a large stick of wood leaning against the water trough. The stick was about three feet long, tapered at both ends and about two inches thick at the middle. It looked like a broken single tree off one of the horse rigs. The downed man staggered to his feet with the wooden weapon firmly gripped for the next charge. The crowd cried foul, but the three-foot-long piece of hard wood came down on the big man's head with a thud.

The crowd surged in unison at this breach of ethics. The man with the wooden club was swallowed up in the angry crowd. A rifle shot fired into the air brought the crowd to heal. Two men could be seen lying in the mud as the circle widened. The big bearded man with the rifle was sitting on one of the loaded wagons outside the circle of men. He barked out some orders to get those two men out of the street and check them out for injuries. His second order was, "Let's get these wagons on to Silverton, now!"

The two mud-covered men were dragged over to the water trough and dowsed with cold water. The report was that the two would be okay, but were in no shape to drive for a day or two. The big bearded man was now standing up and cussing the whole crowd. These wagons are already behind schedule for Silverton. The loss of two drivers created another problem. The wagon master asked for two volunteers to finish the drive. Anyone that could handle four-horse teams would be paid double wages and have a free ride back to this way station in a couple of days.

Clint watched the crowd and finally one hand was raised. Another plea by the big bearded man and Clint raised his hand. A few orders were barked out and Clint was sent over to a nearby wagon. The wagon master asked Clint if he knew how to finish hitching up the four horses to his assigned wagon. Clint grunted that he did.

It soon became clear to Clint that his partner didn't know much about hitching up horses. The man whispered to Clint that he just needed a ride to Silverton. If the wagon master noticed that he didn't have any experience with work horses, he would be left behind. Clint gave the man some instructions and soon the task was completed easily under Clint's experienced direction. Some of the wagons were already headed up the street toward the main road. Clint and his useless helper mounted the wagon and dragged in behind the last wagon.

Horses were Clint's love and he knew how to handle them to get the most from them without causing injury or harm. Clint could tell that he didn't have the strongest set of four horses in this wagon train, but they were plenty capable if handled right. Most of the road into Silverton was an uphill climb, but a few of the valleys in the road were problems. The heavy wagons wanted to ride up on the horses as they came on the down slope. Clint had his helper ride the hand brake on all down slopes. This made the downhill trip much easier for the horses. Clint could see the wagons up in front of him. None of the drivers were helping their horses. Those few downhill rests for his horses made it easy for him to keep his wagon right up to the others. On some of the long up hills, Clint and his helper would walk beside the wagon. This took almost 400 pounds off the wagon which would show up toward the end of the trip.

Three rest stops were held before Silverton's smoke could be seen up ahead. The wagon master had come by briefly to check the horses each time. He would give a nod as the okay signal after each inspection, then head back up the roll of wagons. Up ahead some foul language could be heard as the wagon master chewed out a teamster for not handling his horses right. Right after the third inspection Clint thought he saw a slight smile under the big man's beard as he granted approval and turned back toward the front of the wagon train.

Clint did not want to stand out or be noticed, but horses had to be treated well. The last incline down into Silverton was rather steep. His helper was not a strong man nor was he well-conditioned for steady work. He did try to hold the wagon back off the horses with the wheel brake, but his endurance was spent. Clint wrapped the loose ends of the leather reins around the hand brake and behind the helper's back. This gave some relief to the tired helper's arms as he leaned into the leather straps. A tremble could be felt through the reins as the last energy of the helper was spent on the final decline into Silverton.

Chapter 3

Silverton was a rowdy mining town. The streets were filled with horses, wagons, people and smoke. The air hung heavy with smoke and dust from the ore milling operations. The streets were muddy one day and the next day dusty with a constant smell of horse manure. The sounds of pianos were carried along with the sweet smells of food and beer. The occasional swaggering drunk completed the typical mining town picture. Clint's sharp ears picked up the sounds of cards and poker chips. The thought of games of chance perked up Clint's heartbeat as his mind dwelled on his favorite pastime – poker. He kept telling himself to be patient and cautious. There were at least three men there in this town that had tried to kill him.

Up ahead the wagon master on the lead wagon pulled into an alleyway to the freight yards. The wagons were pulled up side-by-side in a long row. Clint and his helper stood by their wagon until the wagon master came to them. Brief, crisp directions were given to unhitch the horses, remove the harness and brush down the animals. Clint's helper was almost useless, but that didn't matter. The chore was familiar to Clint, and he had plenty of strength and skill to do the job of three men. Once the horses were well brushed, Clint and the helper passed through the green stable doors. The pay clerk was standing beside the wagon master as he approved each payout the clerk was to make. Each man got a $20 house poker chip, plus a slip of paper good for a meal and one night's lodging. If either or both men needed a ride back to the way station, the freight wagons would head back after two nights' rest.

The helper took his $20 chip and meal ticket and slipped away without a word. Most likely he was headed somewhere he didn't have to do manual labor. As Clint watched the man slowly move down the side street, it was obvious his helper was not used to physical activity. The trip had been a lot harder on this softie than would have been expected of a western man. Contrasting the helper's condition, Clint was feeling a lot better. He enjoyed working with horses and physical exertion seemed to boost his well-being and self-confidence. Three full days had passed since his ambush so the soreness was at its peak, but the freight job had helped to keep his mind off the bumps, cuts and bruises.

It was time for his first installment of revenge. The leads to his prey were slim: Six sets of hoof prints that Clint had sketched from memory, one black silver-trimmed flat-crown hat, a set of saddlebags with his gold coins and a new repeater rifle. There was also a small fancy Dillinger pistol that Clint had won in a card game. That small gun would be hard to find even though it was quite unique. It had pearl handles with some Chinese symbols inlaid.

This search for the three attackers assumed to be in Silverton was complicated by the fact that Clint had played a lot of poker in Silverton.

His winnings had obviously been noticed, thus the planned robbery and his planned death. A scheme was needed that kept him out of the gambling houses and bars, but close enough to examine horse tracks and hats. His earlier visits to Silverton gave him a good feel for the town. There was an old stable up one of the side streets that rented horses and was known for the crippled miner that operated the stable. Clint had never used the stable nor met the owner, but he knew about the situation. The old man was able to stay alive by letting drunks and broke gamblers work for their room and board. The two rooms in the loft of the barn were rough, cold and smelly. It took a desperate person to labor in that stable for such poor lodging and biscuits. The offbeat location was just what Clint was looking for. Hard work was what his body needed, and working with horses would be a plus.

The old man was more than pleased to see this healthy well-built man. Clint told the man that he could do all the work if he could have the two rooms in the barn loft to himself. This was an easy deal for the old man because he had not been able to get anyone to take this job for over a month. The entire stable needed cleaning, the corral fences needed repairs, and the few horses that the stable held for rentals looked really shabby. It took only a few hours for Clint to gain the trust of the old man. Clint's skills with horses, coupled with his strength and endurance impressed the owner. The old man stayed in the office and tack room letting Clint keep the stables. This arrangement worked because Clint didn't have to meet any customers and the old man could stay inside off his bad leg and save his back. The rumor was that he had gotten wounded in the Civil War back east.

Operating out of the stable as a downtrodden helper was excellent cover. No one paid any mind to his coming and going as long as the horses were ready and the stable clean. He played the part of a dirty stable hand with very poor social skills. Days were slipping by without any clues concerning his prey. Just about the end of the first week, a glimpse of his black hat passed before his eyes. A fairly well-dressed western-looking man came out of the café at the end of the old stable street. The nice looking black flat-crown hat with plenty of silver trim sat squarely on his head. A few quick steps up the side street to the main drag gave Clint a good view of the man as he turned and entered an office. A casual stroll up the boardwalk past the office provided an even better view of the man. A slow turn onto the street and past the hitching rail confirmed at least two sets of hoof prints that were burned into his memory. The heart gave a quick surge as the tension swelled in his chest and stomach. He heard an audible whisper, ("easy boy, patience, slow down") sneak out of his lips.

He traced his steps back onto the boardwalk past the horses. After a quick reference look to match the horses to the hoof prints he had a man's face and two horses as a good starting place. If he could find the third horse and the other two riders, his mission in Silverton could take shape. As Clint hugged the wall near the street to the old stable, he was almost invisible while still being in plain sight. His old clothes, dirty hands, and shabby look blended into the weathered store fronts. He was just another drifter or bum that dotted this western mining town. Only a few got rich with all the silver and gold ore flowing out of these mountains. The vast majority worked hard and barely made a stay-alive living. The lower end of the spectrum hardly lived at all. They picked up the crumbs to survive, but had no future to look forward to. Clint's image as he leaned against the rough weathered planking of the storefront placed him in the bottom category.

Less than an hour had passed when the gentleman of interest left the office. He turned up the boardwalk toward Clint's position. Without a notice to the bum leaning against the store front, the young man of about mid-30s walked straight past Clint and entered the Grand Hotel lobby about two blocks away. He had left his horse at the hitching rail in front of the Wyoming/Colorado land office.

It was about 30 minutes later when Clint was about to abandon his lookout position when another man left the land office. He gathered up those two horses with hoof marks that Clint had identified. The two horses were led past Clint's position, then into the side street that led to the Grand Hotel stables. The man had a lean and mean look about him. His dress was that of a well-paid guard or gunman. He moved with the agile motion of a cat. This was a dangerous man with most likely superior fighting skills. Clint had developed excellent skill reading people. It was a knack that paid well in poker games, but more importantly it had saved Clint's life many times.

The first man that Clint had identified was more businesslike, but could be a tough adversary. This second man was more dangerous because he looked like a short fuse could trigger violence and death. After both men were in the hotel, Clint ventured into the hotel stable to more closely examine the two horses. He was hoping to find the third horse. While he did find the tracks of the third horse, they were not fresh. The hotel stable only contained five horses, with two of the five belonging to his prey.

A quick look over the two horses and their gear only confirmed Clint's impression. These men were not ranchers nor miners, but gunmen for hire. Their saddles, hardware and clothes - plus better than average mounts - suggested a higher income level than cowboys or working miners. He spent a few more minutes looking over the stables trying to find a link to his ambush. His ears picked up on footsteps coming toward the stable. A big stack of feed sacks provided some cover. Three men came into the main area of the stable. They started saddling up the three horses that did not interest Clint, but the conversation among the men did provide some information. The name Mel Jackson was used several times with authority and fear. These three men must have a deal with this Mel Jackson that involved Cheyenne, Wyoming. They were to get up there as soon as possible to help finish a deal of some type. Clint could not make out the purpose or type of job the three men were talking about. One comment that did come through to Clint was these men's fear of a hothead here in Silverton. Several references to the man alerted Clint to the target they were referencing. This was confirmed when one of the men tapped the black and white stallion that Clint was tracking. He was joking that a stone should be put in that horse's shoe to slow that mean little bastard down. The other rider asked if he meant the horse or Tom Jordan. "Don't be crazy," he answered. "I wouldn't hurt this fine horse; just slow down Jordan to keep him off my back if the boss ever sends him my way."

The third man finally joined the conversation by adding another name to the plot. The boss there in Silverton was called Joe Little. The three men chuckled out loud about that name. It soon came out that Mr. Little weighed over 400 pounds and never rode a horse. His method of transportation was a fancy buggy or stage coach. The light in the stable was not real good but even from his hiding place Clint had a good lock on these three men. Their images were placed into his steel trap memory for future use.

The three men confirmed their schedule out loud. They were headed up north to the "Big J" ranch toward Cheyenne, Wyoming, to join a raiding party of some type. Mel Jackson would send for them when the time was right. Most likely that meant Tom Jordan would be the one sent up there to fetch them. They knew the fat man, Joe Little, would not travel that far, especially on horseback. Another comment by these three riders indicated that the boss, Mel Jackson, was in Durango.

The three men were enjoying themselves, thinking that no one could hear them. They were telling tales on Tom Jordan about his quick temper, savage gun skills and his cheating at cards. They even related the story about some sharp gambler that had taken Jordan for a lot of money at the poker tables about a week ago. Jordan was able to convince Mel Jackson to organize a search party to recover the lost loot. That Tom Jordan had set dynamite charges along the trail back down toward Durango. When this slick-looking gambler came riding by, they had blown him to bits including his horse. The only pieces found were the half-buried horse and gold-filled saddlebags. Jackson had taken the gold on to Durango. Tom had gotten the fancy hat the gambler was wearing when he rode into the blast. The whole side of the mountain went down in a giant rock slide. Matt had found a fancy new repeating rifle where they recovered the saddlebags off the dead horse.

The men saddled up and headed out of the hotel stables. One last parting comment gave Clint another clue. These men were planning to meet up with a Matt in Cheyenne within the week. This had to be the third man that Clint was trying to identify. Clint now knew the two riders and their horses in Silverton, with this third man at a ranch up toward Cheyenne. The ranch had a name of Big J. Clint could only guess that was named after the big man, Mel Jackson, who was in Durango with Clint's gold and saddlebags. Clint examined the hoof prints of the three departing riders but none matched those sketches in his memory. This meant that at least five men here in Silverton, plus the big man called Joe Little knew about the rock slide blast and the supposed killing of the fancy gambler with all the gold coins. If you added the three men that rode south to Durango, which included the possible leader known as Mel Jackson, Clint's adversaries were growing large in numbers.

Clint's anger was most focused on the six men that had been present on the high road when these men had killed a great horse and taken his gold. The two men in Silverton would remain his targets. This Cheyenne activity might bring the man called Matt back through Silverton. If the group was to share in the gold, they most likely would pass back through Silverton on the way south to Durango.

The chores at the stable began to consume a lot of his energy and time. The exercising of the horses did get him out of the town for some fresh air and physical tuning of his battered body. The heavy work around the stable was building his strength. The field trips with the horses allowed him to keep his gun skills at a high level. The real shortcoming of this whole arrangement was the lack of some good poker games. He did miss a challenging game of poker with smart players.

Almost a week had passed since the three riders had left the stables for Cheyenne. The two men that Clint was tracking stayed in Silverton on a regular schedule: hotel, café, bar, gambling and then back to the hotel. An occasional stopover at the Wyoming/Colorado land office completed their typical routine. The name of the second man had finally come Clint's way. The well-dressed man was Paul Wilson, who was Mel Jackson's right-hand man managing the operation up in Cheyenne, whatever that was. No one seemed to bother him. Clint couldn't tell if it was because this Paul Wilson was such a tough hombre or if they were afraid of his mean little side kick, Tom Jordan, the one that had Clint's black hat. Clint would bet it was the mean-looking, small-framed Jordan that everyone kept clear of. However, it would not be safe to misjudge this Paul Wilson. He looked like a businessman in his expensive clothing, but he moved like a physically active hunter or rancher. A good look at Wilson's face one day reminded Clint that he had played this man in some poker games down in Durango. He had observed Wilson from a side street and was sure he had not been noticed. Clint knew that Wilson was as smart as the West had to offer, so caution was his watchword.

Chapter 4

Clint needed a good horse to replace the one that Wilson, Jordan and the other four men had killed. He must be ready to ride ahead if his revenge was to be fully applied. One man, Matt, had already left town with some other riders. The rumor was they were sent up to the Wyoming operation by Mr. Wilson. If it became necessary to seek out this Matt in Cheyenne, it would be a couple of weeks to make a round-trip. That would depend on his finding the man quickly and settling the score without getting himself killed or injured. It would take a really tough horse to make that round-trip without a major break.

Clint had been dwelling on the horse problem for over a week, when into the old stables rode a rundown miner with four beat-up and worn out riding horses. The stable owner and the old man seemed to know each other very well. Clint was given the orders to get the four horses cleaned up, fed and brushed down. If any horse doctoring was needed, then Clint was to take care of that also. Over the next few days the two old men spent a lot of time together talking over old times. It was fairly easy to overhear their talks that roared out of the office and tack room. It was soon clear that the old miner was pulling out. He had done some mining some years ago and made a pretty good strike. He had used the money to buy a small ranch about midway between Silverton and Cheyenne. The two old men shared their stories of when they were both mining just north of Silverton. This was when it came out that the old miner had married one of the bar girls that both of these men had been interested in and teased by.

The marriage was sweet, but the ending was sad. The lady of discussion had agreed to marry the old miner and go with him up toward Cheyenne. The small pot of ore that the miner had found was enough to set the couple up in a little ranch with a small number of cows and a few horses. The two of them had lived an enjoyable life for over five years before trouble set in.

The old miner then introduced the name of Tom Jordan into the discussion. The sad part of the story that was woven by this old miner brought the urge for revenge fresh to Clint's brain. The old miner's two helpers had been roughed up in a poker game with this Tom Jordan. An accusation of cheating was thrown into the game of chance with the results that Jordan killed both of the old miner's ranch hands. No charges were ever filed against Jordan.

It was no more than a month later when his wife and he were driving a small herd to market in Cripple Creek when they were stampeded. His wife was killed and he escaped with a badly damaged leg and shoulder. The herd was lost. It took two months for his leg to heal enough to do some ranching. His spirit was broken and he couldn't do the work on the ranch alone. Jordan so intimidated everyone that he could not find anyone that would help him on the ranch. About two months ago, a Mr. Paul Wilson had come by the ranch with a cash offer. It was one-tenth of what he would have ever considered before his wife died. His options were none, so he sold the ranch to this Mr. Wilson at a fraction of its value. He left there with the small cash, clothes on his back and four horses. The horses were in bad shape because before he had agreed to sell the ranch, his few remaining cows and horses had been driven off twice and almost driven to death. He had spent weeks finding the horses. Now he was headed to Santa Fe where his brother and his wife ran a small store that could use his help. The old miner just needed a little more cash to make the trip down to Santa Fe via stagecoach. Now, if the stable owner could just take the horses off his hands. They used to be good horses before the recent stampedes and all the rough treatment.

Clint had been taking care of the old miner's four horses for the last few days. Although they looked pretty beat up now, these four horses were from good stock. Under Clint's care they could be brought back into fine shape. They would secure his needs for fast and durable mounts. It did not take much hinting about his interest in the four horses before the two old men came to Clint with a fair offer. It was a lot less than good mounts would bring, but Clint did not want to be too eager or show his hand. The old stable owner was a little surprised when Clint brought forth the agreed upon small cash payment. The old miner was happy and departed for Santa Fe a few days later.

The stable owner seemed a little less at ease with Clint after the horse deal. That this quiet stable helper that cleaned the barn for food and a cot would have some ready cash was unsettling for the old man. No words were ever spoken on the subject, but Clint would notice the owner watching him more closely. The man's leg was better and he was beginning to do a little more work around the stables himself. It may also have been that the owner was curious about this young man. Clint had taken some care to hide the gold coin-laden pouch that he had escaped the ambush with. It was a good thing because he could tell that his meager things had been gone through several times after the bargaining for the horses.

To renew his employer's trust, Clint did extra work around the stables. In spite of that, he could tell the stable owner was getting more uneasy with his presence. Maybe the owner was starting to realize what a great horse handler his helper really was. This would then lead to the question of why this able, young, strong, intelligent man was living in his stable. Where did this helper come up with cash? It was becoming time for Clint to move on. A good time for his departure would be when his newly acquired four horses were in top shape. A couple more weeks should do the trick. The second problem was the loss of his good cover job. Operating out of the stable with its closeness to Main Street was a real positive aspect of his stable helper position. No one paid any attention to him as he moved horses in and out of the stables. Also he was trying to keep close watch on Wilson and Jordan. If his third target rider, the man called Matt, was to come back into Silverton, he wanted to be in a position to detect his arrival. The stable job gave him all these advantages. Patience was his guiding word so he would try to sooth the stable owner's concerns.

Clint thought he was making some headway with the stable owner when a new man showed up at the stable. He had worked for the owner the previous year before running off to try his luck at gold mining. He was back and completely broke. The old man approached Clint with the news that this returned man would be bunking in the barn's other spare room. The details of how the two helpers would share the chores would be worked out later. Clint held his peace and rolled with the new development. His decision had to be in his own best interest. Timing might be everything if he was to complete his revenge mission in Silverton. Clint put on his pleasant face and gathered a good dose of patience to pursue his mission on his terms.

The circumstance did not develop as Clint had hoped nor planned, but the time for departing did come quickly. Clint was up early doing his morning coffee at the rundown café just off Main Street. The café windows looked up the narrow street to the side door of Paul Wilson's hotel. It was from this vantage point that Clint's luck came through. Tom Jordan and two other riders gathered around the side door with Mr. Wilson's horse saddled and ready to ride. Clint was really lucky to have been watching as this quick departure took place. Mr. Wilson came out the hotel side door, mounted his big horse and headed north out of town. Tom Jordan and two other rough-looking gun hands followed quickly along with a rush in their look and pace. Clint had hoped to wait it out here in Silverton and catch the missing rider, Matt, when he rejoined Wilson and Jordan. It looked like Cheyenne was his next stop.

Chapter 5

The departure from town had to be slow and easy. The last thing Clint needed was an alert prey. Hopefully, whatever caused the hurried leave of Paul Wilson and Tom Jordan along with two extra gunmen would keep the attention off a lowly stable helper. If this group was headed up to Cheyenne, then Cheyenne was Clint's destination, too.

A good excuse for leaving his stable cleaning job and the sleeping room needed to be logical to the stable owner. His starting arrangement with the owner was that he would handle all the chores and work, but also have the stable loft rooms all to himself. The arrival of the new man had changed that agreement. This alone would be a good reason to be moving on. An extra reason would be his interest in looking for some gold on his own. The old miner had told a good story about his experiences. The finding of enough gold ore to buy a small ranch was worth a try on Clint's part. The old miner's description of the small ranch he had bought and worked for five years sounded like a great location. This was a good pitch so Clint proceeded with it.

There was a slight sign of relief in the owner's eyes when Clint bid his goodbye. Most people would not have picked up on the small telltale sign. Clint's skills of reading faces and body language were sharp from his many games of chance. Without any fuss, he gathered up his few belongings and the four horses. He had gotten two saddles and one pack rack with the four horses. The rack was filled with some gold prospecting supplies to make his story believable. The slow and easy ride out of town completely masked the urgency Clint was feeling inside.

The four riders he would be trailing had a good six-hour head-start. He could cut that distance in half by nightfall by switching off on the other three horses he was trailing. His four horses were in above average condition due to his steady attention over the last month. Clint had judged right about their superior blood line. As the sun set over the high mountain peaks west of him, the cool air settled into the valley. A steady pace had eaten up a lot of the six-hour distance between him and his enemy. He had put in almost an hour on foot to make it even easier for the horses plus keep up his body and endurance building. He had stopped several times to examine the trail but darkness was making that task impossible. The moon was slow in showing up that night so a layover under some low hanging trees was the wise choice. The tender grass around the shaded area was good feed for the horses.

A good four or five hours passed before the bright shine of a full moon put Clint back on the trail. The rest had put some spirit back into his mounts. The roadway was starting a rather steep climb up the rugged mountain side. The road was plenty wide and well used by supply wagons and other travelers. The mining operations north of Silverton were scattered all over the creeks and waterways that bled these mountains of their riches.

A campfire up ahead of Clint put caution back into his pace. The sun would be up in a couple of hours. He needed to see who was in the campsite up front before they saw him. A fairly steep ridge off to the east would be a good vantage point. Tying his horses out of the way, he climbed the ridge with his spyglass in tow. A 30-minute climb provided the lookout spot he wanted. The early dawn was just spreading its soft light into the small valley ahead of him. The campsite was showing some signs of life. It looked like at least six people with two wagons and a half dozen pack mules. It was definitely some prospectors or ranchers and for Clint, that presented a hard choice. He could either go on up the trail passing the campsite or take a slower route and skirt wide around these people. His high vantage point gave a clear view for another mile on up the mountain road. At least two more smoke columns could be seen before the road peaked and dropped out of sight. Clint decided to hold his place and patiently follow at a distance.

The sun was fully on the road up ahead when Clint finally worked his way back off the high ridge. The top most camp that he had spotted an hour earlier was most likely his prey. The four riders had only their horses. The big black horse with some white around its legs looked like the one Paul Wilson was riding. The size of the four men did match up with those that had mounted at the rear door of the Silverton Hotel. The large erect Wilson and the small smooth moving Jordan could be a good match. The distance was too great to make out faces but the size and movements convinced Clint that these four riders were his targets.

Wilson and group broke camp early thus they were still pushing with some urgency. The other two camps between Clint and Wilson were much slower to move out. One of the large groups was headed south toward Clint's position. He quickly moved back into the underbrush and waited for the riders and wagons to pass. This loss of time had cost him almost half the distance he had made up the night before. The slow-moving travelers now between himself and the Wilson group were causing him to fall further behind. When he finally topped the ridge where the mountain road took a long winding descent, the Wilson riders were out of sight. All day long Clint stayed as close as he dared. Night fell and an early camp by the people in front of him provided a chance to slip by without notice. He pushed hard in the dark to make up some of the lost distance. The long downhill slope had a lot of curves so he could not see very far ahead. The last thing he needed was to stumble into Wilson's camp in the dark.

If Clint's memory was correct about the location of the old miner's ranch, he thought he should cross the turnoff in about 10-days' travel. The ranch layout had been described to the stable owner several times while Clint had been eavesdropping. His plan was to leave two of his horses near this ranch then pick them up if he survived the Cheyenne mission. Anyone finding the horses might recognize that they belonged to the ranch and not think anything about their presence. Plus the horses would not stray very far from a place they were used to.

A steady pace all the next five days did not bring the Wilson riders into view. It was late evening when Clint recognized some of the landmarks for the turnoff to the old miner's ranch. A close examination of the trail leading off to the ranch showed two fresh tracks headed down that way. It looked like Wilson's crew had split up. The tracks were neither Wilson's nor Jordan's horses, so they must belong to the two other riders that had come to Silverton for Wilson. Clint knew the old miner's ranch house was only a short distance down this side road. It would not be a good idea to be caught between these two men and Wilson. Proceeding down the side road to the ranch was the better choice.

It was pitch dark when the ranch buildings and the yellow glow of their lanterns stood out in the black background. A few dogs were barking so Clint decided to hold his place back in the trees. Only one man came out of the main house to look around, and then he retreated to the comforts of the house. Clint tried to move toward the ranch building to get a closer look twice, but both attempts caused the dogs to howl. Each time a man would come out and look around. The third time Clint heard the man yell at the dogs to keep quiet. The yell from the house was a curse: If these dogs didn't keep the noise down the man was threatening to either shoot them or turn them loose to chase whatever critter was out there in the dark.

Clint decided to lay low and wait for morning activity. The sun was hardly making its mark on the landscape when three men came out of the bunkhouse. The morning chill was still in the air and the men were not happy to be roused out so early. Five horses were saddled and led up to the house hitching rail. All three men went inside. Clint could smell the morning breakfast. He had been doing cold camps for eight nights so this fresh smell of a hot breakfast was pure torture. He was moving back into the trees when five men came out of the house and saddled up. One of these mounted men went around the barn and herded another four fresh horses to the hitching rails. This only meant that this party was taking spare horses out of the ranch. Although short, the trail out of the ranch to the main road was narrow, except for where Clint was hiding. If he could get out onto the main road without detection he would then be ahead of this group. Caution took charge and Clint decided to stay in the woods with what protection he could find.

The group of five riders and their four trailing horses swiftly exited the ranch. They were mission-driven and had no clue of the stranger in the woods. Clint bid his time before following the group. His curiosity was at a high level but danger dampened his enthusiasm. These five men, plus Wilson and Jordan somewhere up ahead, made for high-stake risks. He turned two of his horses loose after removing their packs and bridles. At least three or four other ranch horses were grazing not 1,000 yards away. His two horses would probably join theirs, but he could easily separate them for his return trip... and that all depended on his survival against at least seven men who were out there somewhere. Clint reminded himself that only three of those were on his revenge list – Wilson, Jordan and Matt.

With only one saddled trail horse now, the going was a lot easier. It did not take long for the dust trail up ahead to focus his mind on the five riders. They were moving at a steady unhurried pace. The four extra horses had neither saddles nor packs, so clearly this group did not have long-distance travel plans. Clint kept his two horses as fresh as possible by switching up every 30 minutes or so. Between the exchanges Clint would jog for 10 to 15 minutes. This method was eating up the distance between him and the group up front. He had to slow down to keep a safe distance. At the next major rise in the roadway, Clint pulled off to one side to seek out a good vantage spot. The spyglass brought the five riders much closer than Clint was expecting when they topped a hill not half a mile north of his lookout spot. The group did not seem to be worried about their back trail. This would mean they thought of themselves as the hunters and not the prey. This attitude would serve Clint well for now.

After the five riders disappeared over the next ridge, Clint moved on north up the road to the next high point. This vantage spot had a great view of a beautiful valley up ahead. Out in the low area near a nice size stream was a cluster of buildings. It looked like a small trading post with a dozen more buildings. Four riders were just arriving from the south. A search back along the trail soon spotted the fifth rider and the four spare horses. They were off the trail to the west nestled in a heavily wooded area. Clint had almost overlooked this hiding place as he scanned the road and valley. Whatever the group was planning, these four spare horses were positioned for a key role. Removing these horses from Wilson's plans might give Clint the edge he would need against a half dozen men.

A single guard was casually watching the extra four horses. A slow descent down the mountain just off the main trail put Clint into the thick timber growth. After riding as close as he dared, his two horses were tied up out of sight. A cautious advance put Clint at the small clump of trees where the lone guard was dozing. The five horses did stir with his movement, but the man slept on in peace. The butt of a gun put the guard under a deeper sleep. The unconscious guard was left to awake without his horses. The five horses were moved on down the mountain and off to the west a couple of miles. There, one by one, Clint released each horse as he moved in a wide arch around the west side of the trading post area. The scattering of the horses took him to the north side of the trading post about a mile out. He then came into the cluster of buildings from the north and headed straight for the run-down saloon attached to the trading post building.

Acting like a trail bum without any particular place to be, he wandered into the saloon. He had not spotted any of the Wilson party's horses either in front of the trading post or any in back of the buildings. Wilson's big black stallion with the white leg markings would be easy to spot. An inquiry about any available side jobs was met with deaf ears. Clint came up with enough money to buy a shot of rye whiskey and drifted off to a corner table to nurse his drink. The table he

selected was close enough to a card table of five
players to hear some of the conversation. These
men were obviously waiting for something. His
eavesdropping soon picked up the names of
Wilson and Jordan and their pending arrival in
the next day or two. This was the information
Clint was looking for, so he eased himself out of
the saloon. Lodging was the next need for a night
or two. A run-down bum was leaning against one
of the porch posts of the trading store. A little
talk and the lodging problem was resolved. The
bum reported on free loft space above the stables
if a person was willing to muck out a stall. The
bad thing about the deal was no smoking nor
drinking in the stable hayloft. The bum said that
only desperate drunks ever took the arrangement
so the livery stable was always open for business.

A survey of the livery stable and its hayloft
confirmed the layout. It would be a good place
to hold up and watch the streets. The heavy rain
clouds that were moving into the valley also made
it a good choice for the night. The stable operator
went over the rules: no booze, and no smoking in
the building. One stall must be cleaned and new
straw put down for each night's stay in the hayloft.
Clint paid his due by hauling out the manure and
putting down fresh straw. He then walked to the
hitching post off the main stretch where he had
left his mount and headed out of town.

He needed to check on the man he had left
out cold back up the trail. Without horses and
with a sore head the man would not arrive into
town for several hours. One more trick had been
played on the man. A boot of his was laid beside
the campfire so the sole would burn off. Given

only one boot, a rough road and an aching head, the man would probably stay put at the campsite. Clint had also taken the time to empty one bottle of whiskey and leave the second one nearly empty. If his buddies found such a setup, they could easily blame the horse guard for getting drunk. The carelessness of letting his boot get too close to the fire and losing all the horses was also likely to cause an uproar. Just as easily, it could be surmised that he had gotten drunk and fallen on a big rock. The knot on his head would confirm that theory.

Clint slowly moved into position so that his strong spyglass could bring the campsite into focus. The man was sitting on a log beside the campfire holding his head. It appeared the man had decided to stay put and not attempt the hike into town on foot. A look around the valley did not find any of the horses that had been led off. This was enough, so Clint slipped away without notice.

Chapter 6

The next two days passed without any action by the four Wilson men. The third day one of the men headed back down south on the trail and returned at nightfall with the fifth man. Clint made a point to find a nearby table at the saloon to overhear the discussion. It was all predictable as Clint had hoped. The guard was found with all the booze gone, a knot on his head and one boot burned up in the campfire. The other men said that Jordan would probably kill him for losing all their horses and drinking on guard duty. It was clear that all five of these men feared the little man called Jordan.

The next morning after mucking out two stalls to keep the livery stable man happy, Clint was on watch duty at the side street café. The young lady who worked there was very pretty and a good waitress. Her coloring and hair reminded Clint of his failed relationship out in San Francisco; he still felt the pain of that loss. Although she was pleasant to watch, nothing was going to interfere with his mission of vengeance. A mid-morning return to the café for biscuits and coffee turned out to be perfect timing. His black hat with silver trim passed his watch point. The man under his hat was tall and handsome, so Clint's question to the pretty waitress was rewarding.

The waitress knew the man to be Matt Tilson who worked for Mr. Wilson. Clint could tell she was rather impressed with this Tilson fellow. That was easily understood. A pretty young lady has few chances to meet a good looking, well-dressed and fully employed gentleman in this quiet place. If her father would only move to Pueblo or Durango, then she would have a better chance to meet a nice man.

Clint had maintained his down-and-out trail bum appearance, so she had not shown any interest in him. However, the easy conversation with her had opened up her discussion about her plight in this small café and town. It was not even a town according to her, but just a trading post, saloon, café, and stables with a dozen shacks. The road through this settlement brought rustlers, cowboys, miners, trail bums and fortune hunters, but few marriageable young men. Clint had a tinge of guilt as he knew the evil in this Matt Tilson that she thought so highly of. The removal of this man from her future would be a good thing, although she would never believe it.

Clint went back to the stable loft for a good position to keep watch on the Wilson gang. A few hours passed before those men split up and rode off in all directions. One of the men came straight toward the livery stables and Clint's hideout. Without a sound Clint moved along the loft floor until he was within hearing distance of the two men below. The negotiations were underway for the Wilson men to buy 10 horses if the stable owner had any. They were willing to pay top dollar for really good saddle-broken mounts. The owner was willing to sell two of his best horses at the inflated price. The Wilson man said the horses had to be ready to ride first thing the next morning. The stable owner would be paid cash when they came to get the horses about an hour after sunrise.

Matt Tilson would have the money and would personally collect the horses. If Tilson was unable to find the rest of the horses they needed, he asked the owner if he knew of any other good ones that might be purchased. The owner pointed out Clint's horse in the side corral. The stable helper might be willing to sell because he seemed to be short of cash. The Wilson man turned to the stable owner after looking over Clint's horse. The owner had no idea that Clint was in the loft overhearing their discussion. He told the man that most likely the stable helper was up at the old café eating biscuits and washing dishes. Horse dealing would be left to Matt Tilson when he got back from the Cross Tree Ranch. If they were short the 10 horses they needed then the helper's horse would be of interest. The Wilson man asked the stable owner not to say anything to the helper about their interest in his horse. Before the man left the stable Clint could hear him climbing the ladder to the loft. A quick squirm into the loose hay allowed the loft to appear empty. The man didn't come all the way up the ladder. A snort of disgust was made and the man left.

Clint knew that the Cross Tree Ranch was northwest of this small town. Matt Tilson was one of the six men that must pay the price for killing his horses and stealing his gold. Not only was Matt one of that group, but he was wearing Clint's special black hat. After the stable owner had retreated to the tack room, Clint was able to slip out the back door and saddle a horse. A wide sweep around the buildings to the trail out toward the Cross Tree Ranch was not noticed. No more than an hour had passed since he left the stable when he came face-to-face with Tilson. A sharp curve in the road and the thick timber stands had completely hid the approaching man. The mutual recognition was instant, with Tilson getting off the first shot.

The horse under Clint quivered and started to stumble off the road. The two drawn guns were not 50 feet apart when Clint's first shot knocked Matt off his horse just as Matt's second shot left his pistol. Clint went head over heels as his horse plunged to the ground off the side of the road. Clint's tumbles let him spring to his feet not 20 feet from his rising opponent. The shot to Matt's right shoulder had made his normal gun hand useless. Still, the gunman was determined to bring another gun toward Clint with his left hand. Another shot into Matt's left shoulder joint stopped everything. Clint had a few bruises but he was okay. The downed man was bleeding away his life rapidly in a lot of pain. The black hat was placed back on the head of its rightful owner. A promise to seek help for the badly wounded gunman in return for information provided Clint with a complete story about the Wilson mission.

Clint bent close as the fading voice relayed the details of a major heist. It took less than an hour for the gunman to bleed out. The dead man's body was dragged off the road over by Clint's dead horse. It was a tough job was to get Clint's saddle and gear off his dead horse. The next task was undressing the dead man. Tilson was almost the same size, build and hair color of Clint. Anyone at a distance would think that it was Matt in his black hat, special spotted goat skin vest and riding his favorite horse. This disguise may come in handy for his anticipated confrontation with Wilson and Jordan. Clint knew he would need every break he could manage. This handling of the first of the six revenge targets had proven way too risky. A split second difference and Clint would be lying back there dead instead of the man named Matt Tilson.

Chapter 7

A new destination for Clint was determined by the dying words of the late Matt Tilson. The Wilson gang was not headed to Cheyenne as announced. A big meeting of two railroad companies was planned near Pueblo and a lot of gold was being brought to the meeting to settle right-of-way disputes. The only pass for the railroads to go west from Pueblo into the lead and silver mines was through a giant, steep gorge. The mountains, a hard rock barrier, were sliced by a single river about 40 miles due west of Pueblo. Whichever railroad company could secure the control of that pass could save a fortune and years of alternate route construction. The story that was presented to Client by Matt had Wilson and his gang extracting a huge chunk of gold as the conflict developed between the two railroad companies. The story sounded shrewd enough to be true.

Clint never looked back as he headed due east toward this reported giant gorge west of Pueblo. He would miss the sweet face and soft voice of the waitress. She would never know what a good deed Clint had done for her.

His new mount was an excellent horse and the saddle was of the finest design. The older saddle off his own horse was tied behind him in a big bundle. He needed to find an additional horse for the mountain travel over this rugged terrain. Matt had gone over to the Cross Tree Ranch looking for extra horses. If he had been successful, then those horses may be located somewhere along this trail. These thoughts had just passed through Clint's mind when off to one side, up ahead, he saw four nice-looking riding stock tethered. A slow scan of the area did not locate anyone left to guard these horses. Clint knew that each of the five Wilson riders had fanned out in different directions to find replacement mounts. It looked like Matt had bought four horses and was leaving them along the trail for the men to pick up on the way to the giant gorge location.

A very cautious approach to the four loosely-tied horses brought no challenges from unseen guards. A smile came over Clint's face as he realized how confident, smug and arrogant the Wilson gang acted. They repeatedly demonstrated their lack of respect for others and never considered that they may be the hunted rather than the hunters.

The best two of the four horses were selected for his extra saddle and bag. The other two were turned loose due to their poor quality.

The two new horses and the excellent mount from the late Mr. Tilson would speed Clint toward the next danger. If his memory of the trail stories was close to right, he could make the big gorge area within a week. Leaving the four Wilson riders behind him was risky, but he should easily out travel them with the three good horses. His campsites would be selected with the precaution against any surprise visitors from the rear. The fourth day of hard riding brought the sight of railroad survey markers along the valley floor.

Clint's extensive reading of railroad news when he was living near San Francisco had informed him about this particular gorge and the fight between the companies. He even recalled that the U.S. Congress had gotten involved with the issue. It was odd that a single mountain pass would be important enough to involve distant government officials. The Civil War had only ended a few years earlier with everyone on the East Coast trying to rebuild the destroyed South and keep the states united. The westward movement of people had relieved some of the political pressure that had boiled over during the Civil War and the reconstruction years. The railroads were already bringing beef from such towns as Abilene and other midwestern railroads to the east. There were big fortunes to be made and greed was the number one by-product.

Clint remembered that Matt Tilson had given him not only a threat, but a new clue. Matt had told Clint that if he let him die, then his big brother would hunt him down. Matt's brother, Luke Tilson, was a top gun hand for the Durango boss, Mel Jackson. Even Tom Jordan did not mess with his big brother Luke. That threat was enough for caution if Clint used the Matt Tilson lookalike vest and horse. Abandoning it quickly seemed a wise choice, but first, it would be used to get close to the gun hands, Jordan or Wilson. It was good to have another name of the gang of six. That left only one more person to identify.

A week had passed since he had left Matt Tilson's body and his own dead horse. The big gorge had to be close if his past readings were correct. The survey markers were fresh and twice he spotted men putting in new landmark monuments and turning points. His traveling had really slowed down in his effort to stay out of sight of any survey crews or travelers. The deeply cut rock of the riverbed was starting to form. He selected a very high campsite with good views down the developing canyon east of his position. It would be a cold camp until he could choose the next move.

His high location gave him the eastern sunrise long before the rays settled into the canyon below. The night scanning of the valley did turn up a halo of lights that could be a town miles up ahead. Also, almost directly below him was a good sized group of freight wagons. Their camp was slow getting started. The one horse in Clint's three that could be identified by Wilson or Jordan was Matt's, so a good place must be found to tether it for future use. It did not take long for Clint to hide Matt's horse and one other.

The descent down to the valley was tricky and dangerous, but speedy. He ended up some distance east of the freight wagons because of their very slow start that morning. A quick camp setup and the appearance of a lone rider overnighting on the trail was staged. Clint had dressed in his worst clothes. His slow movement around his small, cold campsite brought the sympathy he was looking for. The wagon master came over and suggested Clint join his group for the final leg into a town not 10 miles east of his location. With a lot of appreciation expressed, Clint fell into line with the wagons and other riders.

It was late that afternoon when the slow wagon train pulled into a town that a previous surveyor had named Canon. Also called Canon City by some of the locals, it was probably short for mouth of the canyon. No one seemed to know for sure. The late Mr. Gunnison had been killed by Indians a few years after he had completed the preliminary surveys of this area. East of their current location was Canon, the anticipated focal point for building the rail line up the gorge.

Clint had demonstrated his talent with horses in the one day travel with the wagon train. The foreman asked Clint to work with the horses for a few days for room and board. It would be good cover as he tried to figure out what Wilson and Jordan were up to. The freight company had a bunkhouse as part of a large stable and corrals at the edge of town. The corral had at least 30 horses not counting the 16 that had come in with the wagons that Clint had joined.

The next three days were very busy, working with the pull horses and doing some doctoring of the animals. His location at the freight company stables gave him an excellent position to observe the comings and goings of this small but busy town. It was almost sunset the third day when his four followers finally arrived in Canon. They went directly to a boarding house on down the main street past the turn off to the freight company's stables. The four of them sure were a down-trodden bunch. Clint could only guess the thoughts going through their heads as they prepared to meet their boss. A top opening in the stable loft gave Clint a fairly good view of the four having a long discussion amongst themselves before entering the boarding house.

The next two days passed without any glimpse of the four riders. It was midmorning of the third day when a short burst of pistol shots brought Clint to his loft lookout. There stood Tom Jordan with both pistols smoking. Two men lay dead in the dust beside the boarding house hitching rail. A few people were gathering but no one was approaching the man with the two guns. From this distance Clint could not identify the two downed men, but he was pretty sure they were two of the four men that had trailed him into town. It took some time for Clint to sneak down to his gear and retrieve his spyglass. The telescope glass brought Jordan's face into clear focus. The twisted smile on his face told of no mercy nor concern for snuffing out the human lives. The two men in the dirt of the road were definitely two of the four Wilson men.

It was a good 30 minutes before a man with a star on his vest joined the small crowd. Clint watched with complete attention during the short exchange between Jordan and the man with the badge. It was obvious even at this distance that nothing would be done about this shooting. The body language of the lawman told Clint that Jordan was either feared or respected. The entire exchange between Jordan and the lawman didn't last more than 10 minutes. The street cleared, leaving only the two dead bodies lying in the dust.

It was a concern to Clint that Jordan had come into town without his notice. He had kept a fairly constant vigil on the town from the stables, though work with the freight company horses did keep him occupied part of the time. That Tom Jordan was a slippery fellow. His body motion was like smooth oil. Clint had not seen the gunfight, only the results: two men dead, without making a scratch on Jordan. This was no gunman to face by choice.

Chapter 8

Clint's steady surveillance of the boarding house over the next few days revealed little. There was an occasional sighting of Jordan, but no Paul Wilson. It was midday Friday when a heavy buckboard arrived at one of the main hotels, accompanied by a dozen Army Calvary riders. Clint watched with interest as the soldiers carried four big metal boxes into the hotel. This no doubt was the gold that the late Matt Tilson had talked about.

The 12 soldiers did change Clint's thoughts about Paul Wilson's plans. It did not seem logical for Wilson's gang to take on the Army for the gold. There must be some other plan in the works. Over the next few days, at least 10 or more well-dressed businessmen arrived by stage. The big stone hotel was aglow with lights and music every night. Clint's urge to participate in these assured by rich poker pots was almost too much to resist. After all, his number two passion was gambling. It would probably never replace his number one passion of top quality horses and the long-term hope of developing an outstanding breed line.

Clint was still without a clue as to Paul Wilson's plan when the wagon train foreman led two green soldiers into the stable. Their captain had sent them to inquire about horse doctoring. Several of their Calvary mounts needed some treatment for saddle sores and swollen leg joints. The Army veterinarian was back at their base camp. The Army had heard that the freight wagon stables had a man who was good with horses.

Clint's boss was laying on the praise rather thick about his man's skills with fixing horses. It was agreed that a half dozen Calvary horses would be brought to the freight stables for Clint to look over. If it looked like something Clint could handle, then the horses would be left there for a week.

Over the next four or five days Clint learned almost everything about the Army's plans. The green soldiers were openly talking about their mission as if Clint was not even present. Their stories had to be taken with some caution because, as usual, the officers may not have shared all the details with the enlisted soldiers. However, the overall plan was rather clear. The Army was assigned the task of guarding a large gold shipment. The gold was the property of the Denver and Rio Grande Railroad. The federal government wanted the lead and silver mines west of Canon City developed for these metals which were much-needed back east. The carbonate ores up the Arkansas River were rich in lead and silver. The only cheap way to get these mines operational was via rail lines through the Royal Gorge west of Canon City.

Clint was able to take care of the horses within a week as he had promised. There was nothing seriously wrong with the animals, but there was evidence of poor horsemanship and abuse. However, the Army riders seemed quite impressed with the quick recovery of their mounts. If the riders had just stayed off the horses for a week or two, the same results would have been achieved. However, there was no need to share this bit of information with either the soldiers or their captain.

A new piece of information was overheard as the soldiers talked about a planned trip up the Arkansas River basin: A raiding party of Utes was known to be stealing horses along the valley all the way up to Gunnison. The present mining operations about 60 miles up above the big gorge were being threatened, so additional Army troops were being sent to Canon City to stage a rescue operation and retrieve the stolen horses. This planned Army search party was headed right up the canyon where Clint had left his extra horses. If the Army didn't find Clint's horses, then the Utes had probably found them first. Matt Tilson's horse would certainly be a prize find for the Indians.

Clint collected a little extra cash through the freight company's foreman for the work he had done for the Army. Clint knew the foreman had skimmed about half of his money, but cash was not Clint's problem. A week or two off was granted to Clint for his attempt at gold prospecting. This was a good cover story since 90% of the males in and around Canon City were either part-time or full-time gold and silver prospectors.

The sun was just shooting its rays into the mouth of the giant gorge as Clint moved into the canyon. The hard rock walls rose almost a 1,000 feet straight up. The cold mountain water was just above freezing, or so it felt. Fish were abundant; they darted here and there as his horse worked its way up stream. Some places the sheer rock walls were no more than 50 feet apart.

The place that Clint had left his two extra horses was empty. The only signs were unshod prints of Indians. His fancy saddle and his gear were still left undisturbed where he had hidden them. Indian pony tracks were not hard to find if you knew what to look for, but, the hoof prints of Matt Tilson's horse were much easier to identify. After all, six sets of hoof prints from the Silverton rockslide incident were burned into Clint's mind. This slow tracking took Clint right back up a steep incline that he had descended only a short time ago. This was the same trail that he had taken to get in front of the wagon train weeks earlier. His horses were carrying extra flour, salt, beef and his gold coins. His small amount of gold panning supplies was only for show and to match his cover story. The climb up the steep trail was also done very cautiously because Clint remembered what a good lookout post awaited atop the plateau. A constant scan of the river with his spyglass indicated all was clear so far.

Cresting out onto the hard cap rock was somewhat a relief. The sitting duck feeling gradually left as he looked off into the distance from his high perch. A good mile away, moving rapidly, was Tilson's horse and at least six Indians. Tilson's horse stood out even at this distance among the eight or so horses the raiding party was leading. These Indians probably had no idea that a special eye glass could bring them under such close surveillance.

Thinking back over his trip into the big gorge, he recalled two good campsites. If his guess was right the raiding party he was following very likely would join other parties at one of the sites. These

Utes were pretty far away from their home range. They would most likely join with others from their tribe and head on back west as a large band to trail herd the horses.

Clint was about to decide that the risks were too great to go after that one black horse when his spyglass had picked up a dust cloud a good three miles farther west. This could be the other Indian raiding parties driving a collection of their newly-found "free" horses. To Clint's surprise the six Indians leading his horse stopped at the first good campsite. They probably had no idea that their other raiding parties were only a few miles farther west. An elevated rock outcrop gave Clint an excellent view of his black horse and the six Indian raiders. The discussion among the Indians was intense with lots of waving of hands and arms. The Indians' final decision to split up was in Clint's favor, much reducing his risk.

Five riders took off west in a fanned-out search for the other raiding parties. One Indian was left to guard the eight captive horses. The young lonely Indian guard took his time in staking out all eight horses in a long line. He then took a very comfortable position under a low-lying pine tree. Leaving his two horses tied some distance back, Clint moved forward at a snail's pace. The area was very dry so he was careful to keep off any dead wood or twigs to avoid making noise. Stepping from one smooth stone to the next, he was able to reach the tethered horses without waking the guard. He slowly untied his two horses and two others. The guard did turn over twice but did not respond to the sounds the four horses were making.

When Clint got back to his mounts, a quick look back over his trail and the sleeping guard indicated all was still okay. He then tied a bag of flour to one extra horse and a bag of salt and beef jerky to another and turned them loose. A little urging and the two released horses headed back down the first trail toward the sleeping guard. Slowly, Clint moved his four remaining horses along the high rim of the deep gorge below. His heart was beating rapidly from the danger and excitement. This feeling was somewhat similar to a high-stakes poker showdown when everything is on the line. The cold air updraft from the canyon below added a little extra thrill to the feeling.

The next few hours were spent making false trails and tracks in case the Indian raiders decided on trying to recover their stolen horses. A lookout spot was selected off to the south on a high rock pillar. The horses were tied down below and behind this huge mound of boulders. The vantage point gave Clint a good view of both Indian camps. By the time he reached his perch, at least seven or eight Indians had descended on the lonely young Indian guard. Although he could not hear any shouting, the jumping and waving of arms was enough to telegraph the discussion.

It was in the middle of this intense interrogation of the young guard when two other Indians led the two decoy horses into the camp. Clint could only guess at the content of the exchanges as the Indians gestured at the flour, salt and jerky bags, then back onto the poor Indian guard. As Clint had hoped, the entire group finally headed back west. The poor young guard brought up the rear in a completely dejected posture.

Chapter 9

For the moment, the choice facing Clint was how to get even with those two bushwhackers, Paul Wilson and Tom Jordan. The recovery of Matt Tilson's horse was a start. The gun hand, Jordan, would recognize Tilson's horse on sight. He would also recognize Clint from their poker games in Silverton. The many poker hands that Clint had taken from Jordan would still burn in his memory. Jordan would be fairly confident they had killed Clint during the rockslide south of Silverton. A close up face-to-face with Jordan would surely prompt a fast, deadly gunfight. Any slight advantage such as surprise may give Clint his only edge.

The next couple of days on the high mountain plateau gave Clint time for some much needed gun practice. His life may depend on his finest hand gun and rifle skills. Top quality skills are developed or maintained only by constant practice and knowledge. He had to move his campsite each night in case someone decided to investigate all the noise from his target practice.

The sun indicated that it was about midmorning as Clint started his descent off the high plateau. His guns were clean, oiled and ready for action. The highest point of the canyon rim was at Clint's feet. The small deer trail would take him down the steep canyon wall to the water below. A flicker of sun on shiny metal caught his eyes. His spyglass sought out the source of the reflection. A column of 20 to 25 horse soldiers was winding its way through the deep gorge below. The trail had to crisscross the river several times in the narrow canyon. The soldiers were moving slowly as if on a leisurely ride. They would be sitting ducks if those Indians that Clint had narrowly missed decided to raise havoc. A few sharp shooters on those cliffs could decimate the unsuspecting soldiers.

Clint's high position gave him a clear view of the canyon and river trail for a long distance. A slow scan of the canyon walls brought Clint upright in his saddle. About a half-mile up the river were about a dozen or more men moving down the steep slopes toward the river bed. A few flickers of sun reflection told Clint that these ambushers had rifles. The Indians that had been collecting horses had not been carrying rifles. The young Indian that Clint had taken the horses from was probably the youngest of this tribe. The mature fighters would have the few highly valued rifles that were so sought after. A few rifles on these canyon walls above that Army column would be deadly.

Clint's memory went back to his past when he had learned how to shoot long-distance like an artillery gunner. He knew his rifle bullet would travel three-quarters of a mile if properly angled. It would be like arching a ball for a long-distance throw. All he needed was to spook the Indians out of their surprise attack on the soldiers. These Indians were most likely after the top quality horses that the Army was known to have.

A low compact evergreen tree provided excellent cover and shade for Clint. The flat rock cap position gave a clear view of the upstream canyon area. It did not take Clint long to find his target of choice. The Indians had left their horses back up the canyon wall on a large flat area. It was a fleeting thought but he was wondering if the poor young soul he had bamboozled was also left to guard these Indian horses again. It would be ironic but predictable. The young guard's disgrace would keep him out of the much anticipated easy ambush and the glory of capturing 20 or more good horses.

There was no rush as the Army riders were moving slowly toward the hidden trap. Clint set his rifle into a leather sling with lots of patience. His background education in math, surveying and engineering was coming in handy. The knowledge of firearms and his rifle loads was critical in this operation. His past surveying skills helped to adjust for distance and elevation change. The soldiers were still some distance from danger when Clint finished his last elevation estimate.

A slow scan of a small grassy area where the Indians had stored the animals did pick up some motion in the trees at the back wall. It looked like two riders had been left behind to keep the horses. Then, taking the spyglass, he tied it in an easy position for spotting the location of his first shot. A last minute fine tuning adjustment and Clint was ready for his first artillery shot. He had selected the open field where the Indian horses were either tethered or hobbled. The number of Indian ponies must have numbered over 25. That meant a sizeable hunting party was scattered down that cliff front almost on top of the now approaching Army riders.

With spyglass to his eye, he squeezed off the first shot. The crack of the heavily loaded cartridge echoed through the canyon walls. The results of that first shot were sad for Clint as a true horse lover. Out in the middle of the field, in the midst of the Indian herd, a horse reared up and thrashed about. The shot must have injured at least one of the horses. The reaction in that open field was pure panic. The tethered horses pulled loose and started to bolt in all directions. The hobbled horses tried to run with front feet tied together. Several of these horses fell down and thrashed about as they tried to regain their footing. The two Indian guards rode out of the tree line trying to contain the scattering herd.

Clint moved his rifle only slightly with just a small increase in elevation. The second shot hit the rock wall behind the two guards. Just as the two Indian riders bolted away from the sound of the bullet hitting the canyon wall behind them, a lead horse found the exit trail. The loose horses turned almost in unison and followed.

Out of the boulders and cliff below, two dozen Indians were racing on foot toward the remaining hobbled horses. The two guards were trying to head off the exit stampede, but with little success. All told, only about half a dozen horses were left for the 20-plus Indian raiders. The whole group of runners, loose horses and a few mounted Indians quickly vacated the area. Only one loose but wounded horse laid thrashing around in the middle of the deserted field.

It was well over an hour before the first Army soldier emerged cautiously from a large boulder to examine the downed horse. A mercy shot into the downed horse and the event was over. Sadness stayed with Clint for awhile even though he knew that many lives had been saved. Clint held his hidden position until the Army had moved further on up the canyon.

Chapter 10

Sadness was still with Clint the next morning as he contemplated his next move. What he needed was a morale boost. He knew that just northwest of Canon City was a new mining town. Cripple Creek's gambling tables were the first thoughts that came to his head. He had heard some good stories about this wide open town that was host to one of the richest gold strikes east of California. The 1859 gold strike at Cripple Creek was only now being developed due to the area's poor transportation. The railroads were trying to build their lines into that valley, but disputes and fighting were continually holding things up.

The major finds of gold were in hard rock which required refining to extract the metal. The small gold prospectors did not have the resources needed to process the ore. The small miners were selling their ore at 10 cents on the dollar to the organized mining companies. Even at those low prices, money was flowing freely around Cripple Creek, with some even trickling downstream to Canon City.

The freight lines and stagecoaches were making frequent trips between Canon City and Cripple Creek. The roadway was terrible, with narrow passes, rough creek crossings and steep inclines. However, nothing seemed to stop the traffic toward a gold rush. This action was too much for even Clint to resist. He had met several hard rock gold prospectors while working for the freight line stables. Their pack mules and donkeys would need some healing treatment. The word had gotten out that the freight company's young horse handler was good with animals. These contacts had left Clint with plenty of stories about the particular gold rush up toward Cripple Creek.

A constant theme in these tales centered around the small prospector being taken through robbery or at the gaming tables in Cripple Creek. Clint's deep-felt sympathy for the little guy often brought out his Robin Hood tendencies. His love of playing cards in general - and winning in particular - was no doubt the strongest urge driving him toward the Cripple Creek poker tables. Just below that motive was his consistent desire for justice for the weak and the honest hardworking folk.

It took two days for Clint to descend down the high bluff overlooking the Arkansas River's deep gorge and make the long, steady climb to the Cripple Creek poker tables. He had encountered numerous prospector mule trains hauling rock ore to the processing plant outside the town. His many stops along the way at campsites filled in the story. Most of these men had been robbed more than once and yet the dream of getting rich was still a driving force in spite of the danger and their past experiences. Most of them had held in their hands for a short period of time more cash than they could have earned in a lifetime of farming. That cash was then either stolen or lost at the gaming tables before it could be put to good use. Each storyteller had a new plan for his next get-rich moment. They all knew the danger because each and every man could rattle off the names of many dead prospectors. Most of the deceased were men like themselves as they left Cripple Creek with their fortunes.

An accidental meeting with one prospector just on the outskirts of Cripple Creek set Clint's plan in motion. The man had remembered Clint from the freight wagon depot in Canon City. His two pack mules had developed swollen knees. The word was out in Canon City that this young lad at the freight stables could work miracles on crippled animals. Clint's steel memory quickly brought forth the encounter, much to the prospector's delight. Over the old man's campfire that night, Clint agreed to help him move his gold ore money out of Cripple Creek and back up the long trail to his claim and cabin, where his wife and two kids awaited him. The shack of a building was attached to an old mine shaft where he had found good color. He had made two hauls of fairly rich ore down to the Cripple Creek processing plant. Each time he had been robbed of his cash but left with his food supplies. If he could just get back to his wife and kids with the last big bundle of cash in his pockets he would leave this place for good. This story was not new to Clint. How many times had he heard people claim they would change their lives if only they could get out of this or that predicament? Most often when the crisis was over, they returned to their get-rich schemes all over again. A soft-hearted Clint agreed to provide protection and help deliver the cash to the wife and kids back up the rugged mountainside.

William F. Martin

The prospector gave a detailed description of both locations where he had been robbed the first two times. This time the man had decided to camp his first night close to other campers and near Cripple Creek. In the past he was always in such a hurry to get home with his money that he would travel on into the night. The attacks would be almost a day's ride outside of Cripple Creek. Both robberies came as he headed off the main trail and started the climb up the narrow stream bed to his cabin and claim. He would be a good mile off the main road, but still at least another mile from his claim. The gang that had stopped him was comprised of three to five men. He was not sure of the number because only two men were in plain sight each time. Another voice from cover would shout out the instructions to drop his cash and ride on slowly. In their instructions, they would actually tell him how much cash he was carrying, and both times they had been exactly right. If he did not do as they ordered, his cabin would be torched. He never put up any resistance and did as they requested.

As far as he could tell, this last ore load had cleaned out his claim's gold vein. He and his family had to look for another location anyway. If he could collect them all and their meager belongings, the cash from this last load could set them up nicely somewhere else.

Clint presented an idea for the prospector to think about. As payment for his services, the prospector would sign over his claim and cabin. This would be good cover for the prospector as to why he left the claim. The cabin would be a good shelter for Clint as he worked the Cripple Creek saloons. The prospector agreed that the mine now appeared to be worthless, without enough good gold ore to make it worth working. The agreement was satisfactory to both. Clint's job was to get the prospector, his money and his family out safely. The cabin did have one last shipment of about 200 pounds of gold ore stored in bags back in the mine. The prospector was planning on bringing that last cache out with his family and belongings. He had a two-wheel cart and four pack mules back at the mine. His wife could drive the cart and two mules while he was planning on hauling the rest on the other pack mules. Clint could have the extra mules along with the cabin, especially since some of the mules needed some doctoring before they would be of much use.

When Clint learned that the prospector's wife should be waiting with cart and mules packed, he suggested a change in plans. If the prospector thought his wife would let him lead her out of the claim, then Clint would go in alone. The cash could stay with the prospector. The mules would be led up the canyon toward the cabin. If the mules had been fed well in the past, then they would go on back to the cabin on their own. A dummy was made of sacks and the prospector's hat and coat. This train of mules and two horses was led up the trail toward the likely ambush. The past two hold-up locations were clearly described by the prospector. The last turn onto the creek road toward the claim was made with some fear. The bandits may not be that predictable, so Clint took many short stops to scan the rock cliffs up ahead. The trailing animals starting pushing forward as soon as Clint made his last turn onto the trail leading up to the claim. This allowed Clint to turn both the mules and the horses loose with the dummy. They proceeded as Clint had hoped in single file on up the canyon trail toward the cabin.

The prospector had gone over this trail in great detail under Clint's considerable and careful questioning the previous night. There were three or four most likely ambush spots. Riding some distance behind the mules, Clint was constantly looking over the trail up ahead of his decoy. The first sharp curve with high rock walls that Clint had identified as a likely ambush spot passed without incident.

The second danger spot was a double switchback where the creek wound its way between three steep rock outcrops. The spyglass picked up some birds that had been flushed out of the canyon. This warning put Clint on edge with a quickened heartbeat. He needed to get close enough to identify the men but not come under fire himself. The trap, to be really effective, must draw the bandits out of their hiding places. Clint was beginning to think it was a false alert. He had rounded the first curve of the double switchback without seeing any signs of other men. The last trailing mule was just passing behind the next cliff out of Clint's line of sight when a shot rang out. Less than a few seconds had passed when a man leading a horse appeared out of the canyon wall at the curve. He was trying to mount his horse in haste when the prospector's horse and the dummy came barreling around the bend past the bandit. The man sent two shots after the speeding horse, then mounted and started the pursuit. Two other riders came into Clint's view as the dummy passed his hiding place. The three bandits were sending a hail of bullets at the fleeing horse. One or more of those shots hit their target. The speeding horse and its load of grain sacks, coat and hat crumbled into a giant cloud of dust.

The sound of injured horse squalls made Clint's horse prance around and send some rocks down onto the trail in front of the oncoming riders. They immediately sent bullets Clint's way. Without hesitation, Clint's rifle dropped one rider after another in his tracks. The silence was intense as all three men and the prospector's horse lay dead in front of Clint's vantage point.

The time dragged by as Clint hugged a big rock and stayed put. If there were more bandits they never came out of hiding. It was over an hour before Clint ventured out of his hiding place. The dead horse was stripped of its gear and the dummy prospector. The three dead bandits were searched and all guns and ammo put into the saddlebags.

The three bandits' horses were trailing behind Clint's horse as he approached the cabin. The shootout had no doubt been heard by the wife and two kids, so the next step could be dangerous. The mules were milling around the corral trying to get to the feed trough. No one had come out to let them in or separate them. Some distance from the cabin, a big boulder gave Clint some protection. It took several calls to the cabin before he got a response. A rifle barrel sticking out an open window was accompanied by a women's voice. It took a long time for Clint to convince her that her husband had sent him. The three bandit's horses were the final proof that broke the icy standoff.

Clint was given permission to move closer and let the pack mules into the corral. This put Clint close enough to talk through the scheme that he and her husband had planned to get her and the kids out of the canyon. As he went through the details and revealed his knowledge that she was to have the two-wheel cart and pack mules ready for travel on his return, she finally yielded.

It took almost no time for her to do the final packing. The heavy bags of gold ore were lashed onto the pack mules. The kids were about eight and 10 years old. They proved to be quite experienced in handling the difficult mules. The family seemed very pleased to be leaving this remote cabin behind. The hard work of mining and the rough mountain living had worn hard on the woman. Clint could tell that under that weather marked face and hands, there used to be a very attractive young lady. She did not show any signs of regret or disappointment. The woman and both kids were only talking about better times ahead and new adventures to come.

Their arrival back into the prospector's camp was a delight for Clint's heart. The family was safe and sound. They had all their money and a few bags of gold ore as well. They would not let Clint leave the camp until she had fixed all of them a big dinner. It was rather late before all the excitement settled down. The final thrill that night was the return of the husband's jacket and hat. There were two big bullet holes in the jacket and one through the hat. It was a clear reminder of how dangerous the task had been. All of them, even the kids, made a lot of jokes about their dad's jacket and hat. It was a way of dealing with the possibility that he could have been killed.

The next morning found a more sober camp. It became clear to the prospector that the robbers had known about his cash and the exact amount each time. This could only mean that someone in Cripple Creek had inside information on the gold ore payouts. Clint suggested the family head directly down to Canon City and cash out there instead. One more night on the road should put them in Canon City. The prospector and his wife had made several trips down there over the past three years. They were familiar with the road and layover places. This seemed a much safer option than going back into Cripple Creek. The family of four wasted no time heading south to Canon City.

Chapter 11

As the new owner of a prospector's cabin, mules and an empty gold mine, Clint decided to check it all out before embarking for his much-delayed gambling fun. The cabin was in fairly good shape with cast iron cook stove, tables, chairs, and feather bed. This was a lot better than sleeping on the ground. It also had an added feature that was a complete surprise: water. The cabin was built over the entrance to the mine. The back room of the cabin opened directly into several large mine chambers of solid rock. The ceilings were dug out in dome slope and did not require any roof bracing. Along one side of these open rooms ran a small stream of water. Someone had put some pipe in the trench and this carried the water to the cabin. A small steady flow of cool, clear mountain water fell into a kitchen basin. The overflow then proceeded down a rock groove to watering barrels in the corral. For Clint, a mountain shack with running water was just about a miracle.

The overflow water from the corral followed a trench past the chicken coops, then into the open pasture area. A good stand of green grass covered the hillside a fair distance down the slope. This whole geographical area was somewhat semi-arid except for small stream beds and a few wet-weather springs. The water tapped inside the mine appeared to run year-round. With a source of water the prospector and his family could have made a decent living by ranching and farming their land. Gold had a way of clouding the thinking of most people. The get-rich mindset often leads a person away from a steady work pace that could pay out more in the long run. Clint just marveled at this nice setup. The prospector and his family had walked away from all of this because the elusive gold ore had run out.

Clint spent an extra two days fixing up a few repair items and doctoring the animals. Just enjoying the peace and quiet was refreshing. This time allowed him to replace his bullets with his loading kit. The horses were rested and ready to ride. At last, it was time for some fun. The ride into Cripple Creek took him past the shootout spot. The wild animals had taken their turns on the dead horse. Clint had put the three dead bandits into a shallow grave with lots of stones on top. That site did not seem to be disturbed. Riding past the gravesite did dampen his enthusiasm for fun at the gaming tables.

He had a lot of thinking to do before riding into Cripple Creek. The prospector had recognized Matt Tilson's horse as one that was frequently seen outside the Cheyenne Palace. The prospector knew Tom Jordan by sight. He had reported seeing the rider of the black horse that Clint was riding as a regular visitor to the Cheyenne Palace and Jordan's table. Another player at that private table was the Cheyenne land office manager, Paul Wilson. The land office kept a suite in the Cheyenne Palace with an entrance off both the main lobby of the hotel and the back alley. It was rumored that the Cheyenne land office owned the Cheyenne Palace as well as some land up toward Canon City and Cripple Creek, plus a big ranch west of Durango.

The piece of the puzzle that Clint needed to find was how the bandits were getting the information on the size of a prospector's cash payments. These robberies seemed too well planned and timed. Riders could not stake-out all the canyon roads outside of Cripple Creek on the chance of finding cash on individual riders. These bandits had to know in advance how much cash the prospector was leaving Cripple Creek with and when. It was Clint's hunch that his investigation would eventually lead him to Paul Wilson and his gun hand, Tom Jordan. The tie-in to the assayer's office where gold ore was traded for cash could be a key piece of this puzzle.

The prospector had told Clint about the freight company's yard, stables and bunkhouse in Cripple Creek. Clint was aware of this setup from his days with the freight company in Canon City. It was late evening when Clint finally arrived at the outskirts of Cripple Creek where the freight company had its complex. His arrival did not cause any commotion because several of the muleskinners knew the young lad from the Canon City stables. He was immediately assigned a bunk and given a free meal ticket for the small café across the street.

Clint's plan had finally settled in his head as he took a small corner table at the café. He had pulled the prospector's jacket with the two bullet holes out of his saddlebags. The prospector's wife had given it to Clint both as a joke and to remove reminders of that near-death experience from their lives. This jacket had some very unique features, such as deerskin mixed with bearskin along with some Ute symbols on the chest pieces. In fact, when Clint rode into the freight yard, one of the muleskinners instantly recognized the jacket as the prospector's. The blood stains from the horse were still visible even though the jacket had been washed thoroughly. Clint was ready with a story that went with the jacket, blood stains and bullet holes.

Clint had barely gotten seated at a back corner café table when his breath was brought up short. Coming toward his table was the pretty young lady, Betty, from the trading post back toward Silverton. This young face was the same one that he had talked to often about her boyfriend, Matt Tilson. She came to his table with napkins, water and utensils. Her big smile reassured Clint that she knew nothing about his killing her boyfriend. She quickly spilled her story to him as if they had been long-lost friends. It turned out that the Ute Indians had started raiding all along the trail around her old trading post. The Army had come by a couple of weeks ago and escorted anyone that wanted to leave the area to Cripple Creek or Canon City. She had decided on Cripple Creek because her aunt ran a boarding house there and Matt Tilson had mentioned this town on numerous occasions. She had not heard nor seen anything of Matt for almost a month.

Her aunt was glad to provide a room and meals in exchange for her help with the boarding house. She was working the dinner shift to get spending money. Her life here in Cripple Creek was a lot more interesting than her prior situation at that remote trading post. First off, there were a lot more available young men. She confessed that she was interested in a couple of young gents, even though her thoughts often went back to Tilson. This reference to her old boyfriend gave Clint the opportunity to plant his rumor. He told her that Tilson's horse had been recovered from a Ute Indian raiding party only last week. The horse was out at Clint's newly acquired cabin just west of Cripple Creek. Clint suggested that she should move on with her life since it seemed the return of Tilson was very unlikely. She was sorry to hear the story, but she had already gotten used to the idea that he wasn't coming back for whatever reason. She quickly changed the topic and took his food order.

Clint took his time over his meal for the next hour. He did catch Betty looking his way several times. It would only be natural that her curiosity would be at a high level. His identity when near her trading post had been as a stable bum mucking out stable stalls for a place to sleep in the barn. They had had several friendly conversations back there even though he was just a dirty drifter without money. Now he'd shown up in Cripple Creek with an apparent job at the freight company. Clint knew he was well-built and had an excellent education, if you looked under the dirt and shy behavior. He had to keep Betty from getting too much insight into his true self. He did not need any personal complications as his search for revenge continued.

The café's location did get Clint into a back-room poker game. The players were workers and worn-out miners just looking for some fun. The money was not of interest to Clint at this time... only information. His card skills kept the winning pots evenly spread around the table. These players had lots of rumors which intrigued Clint. They all knew Wilson and Jordan by sight and reputations. The other players made a point of warning Clint to avoid the mean gunfighter Tom Jordan. He was a well-known cheat at card playing who had killed several men in cold blood when they called his hand. Jordan often hung out with another Cheyenne company employee, the good-looking Matt Tilson. None of the card players had seen Tilson for a month, but his horse had reportedly been seen at the freight company yard.

This reference to Tilson was the opening that Clint needed to further spread his rumor. Casually, he explained that Tilson's horse had been recovered from a group of Ute Indians out west of Canon City less than two weeks earlier, and that he had personally captured that black horse with white leg markings, along with a couple of others. By Clint's account, Tilson's fine saddle and gear had been found still on the black horse. The story brought immediate alarm to the poker players. If Tom Jordan learned about Tilson's horse, he would most likely kill first then ask questions later. All the poker players expressed fear for Clint's life as well as their own. The group strongly suggested that Clint turn that black horse loose as soon as possible, and that he should avoid Jordan by getting out of town without spending another night in Cripple Creek.

As the poker game ended, the other players slid some of their money into the center of the table to help fund Clint's immediate departure. They drifted out the exits so quickly that Clint was soon left sitting alone. Rumors in a small community are like wildfire in a dry forest. This report that a gambler in the back-room of the old café had Matt Tilson's horse hit Cripple Creek faster than lightning. While Betty did not normally serve the back poker room, she came back anyway to warn Clint. Real fear was in her eyes when she said that Tom Jordan was coming down the street. Now, there was no question about his mission.

Tom Jordan came through the door of the café that led to the poker room. His guns were drawn as he walked a few casual steps up to the back of the single card player. The room was empty except for this one man sitting with his back to Jordan. The card player was shuffling the deck as if in complete peace and sobriety. This whole setup was such a surprise that Jordan lowered his guns and stepped right up behind Clint's chair.

Clint, in a slow, calm voice, then uttered the most unexpected message. The boss, Mel Jackson, had sent him to find Paul Wilson and Tom Jordan. Was the man behind him either of those two gentlemen? The split-second that Jordan used to think about this message was all the time Clint needed. Clint slammed his chair back against Jordan, pinning his half-drawn guns downward. Two slugs tore through Jordan's body as he staggered backwards. His guns discharged harmlessly into the floor. The gunpowder smoke was still hanging in the air when some heads from the café looked into the back gaming room. The only occupant was a dead Tom Jordan.

Cripple Creek just about came unglued with the excitement around the death of a hated gunfighter. Clint slipped in his story amidst all the excitement and confusion. This falsely spun account caught on quickly and spread like no true story ever would. The tale was that the poor muleskinner was sitting alone at the card table. The door from the café sprung open with Tom Jordan standing there with both guns drawn. Almost simultaneously, the alley door was flung open with at least two gunmen shooting Jordan. The muleskinner crawled out of the shootout on his belly without anyone paying him any mind. Without any witnesses, this tale spread like wildfire with everyone looking for the two shooters. Jordan was so fast it had to be two or more men to take him out.

Clint held up behind a stable watering tank displaying real fear. A couple of the card players that had left him in the café backroom soon sought him out. They were glad that he had escaped with his life. The apologies were freely flowing now that the feared gunfighter Jordan was dead. Everyone wanted to know what the shooters looked like. Clint's believable reply was that he was lying flat on the floor and didn't see anything. A small crowd gathered then surged toward the nearest saloon. Drinks were flowing freely as the story of the shootout gathered steam and size.

Betty soon found Clint and gave him a big hug with tears in her eyes. She knew he should have left the gaming room when everyone else had. She reminded Clint that she had warned him that Jordan was coming down the street. Clint then played his fear response, saying he was so scared, he didn't know what to do. He was going to escape out the alley door, but heard noises out there. It was his thinking at the time that Jordan had decided to come into the gaming room from the alley. Clint had decided to crawl to a side closet and hide when the café door sprang open catching him in the middle of the room on his hands and knees. This tale brought the raised eyebrows response that a coward's story brings out of the strong, brave, western attitude of onlookers. Clint could see that response in Betty's eyes as she tried to console this frightened young man. This was just what Clint wanted. No one would suspect a frightened young muleskinner to stand up against the mean, fast Tom Jordan. People soon moved away from Clint with an occasional drink sent his way on grounds of pure sympathy. Even lovely Betty soon slipped away into the crowd.

The rumors were running wild about Paul Wilson and his men. What would they do without their main gun hand? The story was finally pieced together that Wilson and his men had headed down toward Canon City for a big meeting. Jordan had returned to Cripple Creek to follow up on the sighting of Tilson's horse. When it was learned that the young muleskinner at the freight yard had the horse, Jordan set out to find the man and learn how he had come by Tilson's horse. The rest of the story was now history.

Clint gathered his supplies, horse and gear from the freight yard bunkhouse and headed out to his claim and cabin. He needed time to let this all settle before his next move. His revenge was now satisfied for two of the six killers he sought.

Chapter 12

The prospector's cabin was a peaceful retreat from Cripple Creek. Clint kept himself busy with chores to calm his brain. The elimination of Tom Jordan so easily was lucky, and it all came about due to some quick thinking on Clint's part. Tom had the reputation as the fastest gun hand in Paul Wilson's group. The story about Wilson himself was almost blank.

The reason that all these gunmen were being brought to Cripple Creek and Canon City was still unclear. The soldiers had escorted a load of gold to Canon City while Clint was down there. The older rumor that Paul Wilson, too, had moved his men to Canon City would raise the possibility that the get-rich scheme was centered in or near that city.

The position of Matt Tilson's horse would bring attention and thus danger toward Clint. The black horse would need to be used in a way that would distract Wilson and his men. There was a chance that the shooting of Tom Jordan by unknown men could spook Wilson. After all, the story back in Cripple Creek was that he had been sent back to investigate the sighting of Tilson's horse. That mission had gotten him killed. The story out of that incident hinted that a cowardly stable hand was present during the shootout. The story had the man hiding on the floor and not seeing anything. Just the fact that this young muleskinner was in the back room of that café would be suspicious to Paul Wilson. If Clint was to show up with Tilson's horse and the vest of the ambushed prospector, the surprise might be an extra edge. The real problem was getting close enough to Wilson without being killed by one of his men.

The mission or job that Wilson was planning must be brought to light, and that could only happen closer to Canon City. Leaving this small cabin with its fresh running water in a remote, quiet canyon was difficult. Regardless of the sacrifice or his past, Clint had to carry through on his revenge mission. Six men had killed his horse, stolen his gold and assumed they had taken his life. In these circumstances, Clint felt justified in being the jury, judge and executioner.

The high cliffs around the western part of Canon City provided a good vantage point to sit, watch and plan. Tilson's horse, vest, and other gear were stored some distance away, ready to be put into play. It took less than a day of constant surveillance to locate Paul Wilson and several of his men. Wilson was staying in the best hotel in the city. The Wilson men were back at the same complex where Clint had first spotted Tom Jordan. This high perch outside of Canon City was not nearly as good as the freight company stables lookout. It would probably be common knowledge that the young muleskinner from those stables below was the same man that had witnessed the shooting of Jordan up in Cripple Creek. This made the risk too high to venture into the city.

The second day of consistently watching the streets of Canon City did bring a surprise. A well-dressed couple and two kids boarded the stage bound for Denver. It was the prospector, his wife and their two boys. Even from this distance, Clint could tell they were leaving for good. The departing did not seem to be related to the Wilson men in any way. This helped Clint to surmise that the Paul Wilson men did not recognize the prospector and his family. It was a guess, but with all the new clothes and a ticket out of town, that prospector had probably escaped with a lot more gold than he had led Clint to believe. Good for them... and Clint was happy with his depleted gold mine up toward Cripple Creek. The solitude and cozy setting with plenty of water was a place that Clint could see himself spending a lot of time. But first, revenge was on his mind – and Paul Wilson was the only one left of the three who had ridden north after killing his horse and stealing his gold.

The third day of watching the Wilson men did pay off. A group of well-dressed business men met with the Army officer and the gold escort crew. The entire group went into the large stone bank building. It was less than an hour later when the Army officer and his men departed Canon City. The businessmen soon left the bank building and joined another group of men waiting in front of the fancy hotel – the same hotel where Clint had frequently seen Paul Wilson. At this distance, there was no way for Clint to even guess at what was going on below. One thing for sure: Whatever Wilson had been planning was going to happen soon.

It was late afternoon when Wilson's men pulled out of town. There were at least eight men, including the two leading six mules. They took the road east out of town. The Army riders had left in that same direction much earlier. To Clint's surprise, he spotted Wilson walking the boardwalk between the hotel and the bank with three or four of the well-dressed businessmen. They turned into one of the best restaurants in Canon City. It was only a guess, but most likely Wilson was making his alibi with the very men his crew was going to rob.

This scene unfolding below was intriguing, but it was not his main interest. Wilson was his prey. His target did not emerge from the restaurant until at least two more hours had passed. Even from this distance, with the aid of his spyglass, it was clear that the businessmen and Wilson were in good spirits. They turned into the saloon doors of the fancy hotel, most likely for a game of chance. The very thought of a good poker game with rich businessmen raised Clint's heartbeat. The chill of the evening was just beginning to penetrate the air. The perch high in these cold boulders was a sharp contrast to the warm comfort of a fancy poker table in the best hotel in town.

Clint was trying to decide if he should move in closer as night drew near. His line of thinking was interrupted by movement at the side door of the bank. Four mounted men, plus two others operating a small wagon were leaving the bank. The side window of the bank had been lit-up ever since the sun started to drop behind the western mountains. When the wagon and its escort pulled away from the bank, the lights went out. The street lights showed Clint the movement of three men. After they left the bank side door, they headed up the street to the hotel. One of the men went into the same saloon entrance that Wilson and the other businessmen had taken. It was not much of a leap in reasoning to understand that the businessmen were being informed that the gold shipment was on its way.

Clint could just hear the surprise in Paul Wilson's voice when some time in the future word would reach the group that the gold shipment had been robbed. Wilson would hang around the group and express his outrage at this lawless land. After a limited time, Wilson would gracefully dismiss himself and head back west. What Wilson didn't know was that the assumed dead Clint would be waiting for him.

Chapter 13

The shelter that Clint had chosen was the barn of the enemy. The guard dogs of the ranch house had slowly been made into friends. The lonely guard at the ranch had been spooky the first couple of days that Clint had been sneaking around the place. As the dogs learned Clint's scent and enjoyed the fresh meat he was feeding them, all turned peaceful and quiet. It turned out that the dogs preferred the company of Clint over the crude, mean treatment the Wilson man was dishing out.

The horses Clint had left behind plus the ones he had from Cripple Creek were well fed and rested. Almost a week had passed since he had seen the gold leave Canon City. If his insight into Wilson's activities was anywhere close to being right, either Wilson or his gold cache should be arriving at this remote thieves' den soon. The trap was set if only the mouse would come home.

A steady rain had set in for two days. The barn loft was a very comfortable dry place to spend his time. Daily trips out to check his horses and set a few extra surprises kept him wet, busy and active. A change into dry clothes was always welcomed. The Wilson man in the main ranch house never came out to do any ranch maintenance. The cattle and horses were left to roam on their own. Clint did not expect to see him out again until the sun came out or Wilson showed up.

It was the Wilson gang and the pack mules that arrived first. There were only seven men and two had some injuries. The group led the pack mules into the barn right under Clint's hiding spot. The ranch house man came to the barn and helped with unpacking the mules and getting the two wounded men to the house. His ear close to the loft floorboards gave Clint the whole story.

Wilson had given them an excellent plan. The gold guards were caught by complete surprise just 20 miles outside of Canon City. The gold was intended as a major transaction between two railroad companies for the right-of-way through the gorge. One of the major ranches in the area had offered his home as the meeting place for the gold transfer. The Army had cleared out because these business deals were private business. Wilson had figured out the whole scheme to perfection. The ambush site was about midway between Canon City and the ranch transfer site, just one day's travel outside Canon City. There were two favorite overnight trail spots at the one-day travel time. Wilson had predicted that the men transporting the gold would pass the first stop but camp at the second.

The Wilson gang was ready and waiting when the gold wagon arrived at the second camp site. The Wilson men had been told to wait until the camp was completely settled, the meal eaten, and the bedrolls occupied. The single guard was dropped first and all the other guards and the driver were killed before they got off a single shot.

The ranch hand asked, "If that went off so slick, then how did these two men get wounded?"

That story was quite odd. Wilson had told them to take the mountain trail with pack mules around Canon City and bypass the gorge even though it would take them two extra days.

The second day around the gorge pass they had settled into an overnight camp. It was just before sunup when a dozen Indians attacked them for their horses. The shootout killed at least four Indians but one of their own men got killed. The other two wounds were not too serious but caused slow travel over the rough mountain terrain. One of the pack mules and one horse was lost in the raid. The men had brought back a lot of the Indian gear to prove to Paul Wilson that they had truly been attacked by an Indian party. Clint could hear the fear in their voices as they explained the raid and the loss of one mule and its load of gold.

The barn went silent as the men headed to the ranch house. It was not long before the sounds of men drinking and arguing came from the ranch house. This gave Clint the opportunity to examine the mules and their packs right under Wilson's nose. The mule packs were loaded with freshly minted $20 gold coins from the Denver Mint. These were one ounce coins that could be spent anywhere. After lifting several of the mule packs, Clint estimated that each mule was packing about 200 pounds of gold.

This gold robbery had probably netted close to a quarter million dollars in gold coins. The Indians had gotten away with at least $50,000 of value on the one mule. At least $200,000- worth of brand new gold coins were lying on the barn floor in front of Clint.

His amazement was broken by a ruckus on the porch of the ranch house. He reached a crack in the barn planking to look at the men on the porch. The shootout between two sets of four Wilson men was at close range and deadly. Three of the men were on the ground almost immediately, but still shooting each other. While this rampage seemed to last forever, Clint was sure the outburst lasted no more than 30 seconds. Eight men with 16 or more weapons between them left all eight wounded. The only two standing had even emptied their sidearms and were standing not 20 feet apart looking blankly at each other. Two or three of the wounded men on the ground were still moving and yelling for help. A moment of sanity came over the two upright men. Three of the downed men were helped into the house. The rest lay still in the cold dirt as their lives drained out of them.

Clint stood in a frozen position as his brain processed what had gone on before his eyes. His ears picked up another wave of loud shouting within the house. One of the men came out yelling over his shoulder that he was taking his share. He was getting out before Mr. Wilson got there to doubt their feeble story of an Indian raid. The man turned and headed straight toward the barn. Whatever his wounds, they did not keep him from walking briskly toward the barn doors. Another Wilson man with a rifle came onto the front porch and shot the departing man in the back. Clint could see his chest explode as the large caliber bullet exited his body. Clint's rage at the man shooting one of his own in the back was too much to contain. One single shot from Clint's rifle dropped the man on the front porch. All fell silent as Clint waited for any response from within the ranch house. The silence dragged on forever it seemed. Finally, Clint left his hiding place behind the large barn doors. A slow sneaking pace up to the ranch house side window gave Clint a nightmare view. Blood and bodies lay on the floor just inside the front door. There was no sign of life within the ranch house.

Chapter 14

The sound of fresh running water was like music to Clint's ears. He slowly rolled out of his cot, stoked the fire in the iron stove, and put a coffee pot on the cast iron cook top. Life might be short for him, but right now, this very moment it was as good as it gets. He was in his own place... the prospector's mine and cabin. This depleted mine now held $200,000 of freshly minted gold coins, and some of the richest poker games east of San Francisco lay not more than a day's ride into Cripple Creek.

A week had passed since he had witnessed the self-destruction of Paul Wilson's gold ore-steeling gang. Clint was feeling rather bold and lightheaded as he recalled what he had set up. This boldness did not distract from Clint's daily gun practice and physical fitness regimen. His body was as finely tuned as it had ever been. The threat of danger he had set up for himself was real and he knew it deep into his bones. The natural fear of being hunted did not keep an occasional light moment from flashing through his mind.

A full bag of gold coins and two fresh horses made the trip to Cripple Creek gambling tables truly exciting. The muleskinner was returning to the city where many people knew the story of his crawling out of the saloon back door after Tom Jordan's death. The reputation of being a coward travelled faster in western cities than a snow avalanche down a mountainside.

His nerves were on edge as danger could lie around any corner, down any dark alley or through any doorway. This situation was mostly of his own making. Even as a chill went through his bones, a slight smile came to his lips. He might have been too smart for his own good, but the plan was in motion.

It was Friday evening just after sunset. The street lanterns had been lit and the music was starting to overflow from the batwing doors of the saloon onto the boardwalks. Clint's muscles were tight but he was looking forward to playing his favorite hobby – poker. To set the stage, a good steak at his favorite café should do the trick. The pretty little waitress Betty would be good to see, even though she thought of him as a poor muleskinner and a coward.

The café was only half full and Betty spotted Clint immediately, but turned away. The older lady came to his corner table for the food order. She brought hot coffee and a half loaf of fresh baked bread with a big slab of sweet butter. The fresh coffee was a good start as Clint settled into his out-of-the-way table. A few rumors were floating around at the other tables, but no word about Paul Wilson. The huge steak arrived so Clint concentrated his attention on the magic taste of a perfectly cooked hunk of beef. He killed as much time as he could without drawing any attention to himself. He was just getting ready to leave his table when three men came in talking about an Indian raid west of Canon City over toward Silverton. Two of the men were stage drivers that had just finished the run from Durango through Silverton and Canon City to Cripple Creek.

The whole restaurant got to buzzing about the Ute uprising and a gold robbery. The story started with the two railroad companies reaching an agreement on the right-of-way access, through the Royal Gorge. There were reports that almost half a million dollars in gold was stolen, just before the transaction could be completed. Some Ute Indians were later trapped with one pack mule carrying some of the gold. Then a week later, a Ute raiding party attacked Paul Wilson's ranch out west of Canon City and killed all the ranch hands. Only a small portion of the gold was ever recovered. The U.S. Army had been sent for to track down the outlaw band of Utes. A dozen men had been killed by this roving band of Indians over the past week or two. Betty then piped in that she had to leave their trading post over toward Silverton because of those raiding parties.

Clint wondered to himself how many other incidents the Indians had been blamed for when they knew nothing of the reasons. This gave Clint a sad moment because his scheme had falsely pointed the finger at the unsuspecting Indian hunting party. The Army would be relentless in pushing the Indians out of their own territory. The murder of a dozen white people would pressure the Army to extract a heavy toll. There was already a lot of pressure from the U.S. Congress to move the Indians off the land where gold and silver had been discovered. The Treasury needed the money and the westward migrating people were greedy for land.

Clint had left the restaurant without even an interested glance from the pretty waitress. It did hurt his pride a little, but he had chosen the coward label rather than taking the hero name for gunning down the mean, fast gun, Tom Jordan. He could now walk around Cripple Creek as an unnoticed person. No one would fear him. Thus, he could get into poker games easily with a little flash of money. The rich, shrewd and bold would love to take money from a weak character. The card sharks would pounce on one without fear of challenge for their tricks. This was an ideal setting for Clint to extract a healthy sum from crooks... but this time, that was not his intention.

Wilson's return could occur at any time if Clint's baiting really did work. The next two days, all through Friday and Saturday nights Clint spread Wilson's gold coins freely throughout Cripple Creek. He was soon welcomed at any poker table as the rich sucker with plenty of money and very poor luck.

The local lawman did corner Clint late Saturday to find out where all these gold coins he was losing had come from. The ready-made story easily poured out of Clint's mouth without any hesitation. Some Indian traders had bought some of his horses with newly-minted gold one-ounce coins. As he explained to the deputy, he was not aware of any gold robbery when the horse trade was made. He, himself, had just heard of the railroad gold heist at the café Friday night. He asked the deputy if he had been in danger dealing with the Indian traders. The lawman dismissed Clint with a show of contempt. It was obvious that the deputy had heard about the cowardly way this young muleskinner had acted a few weeks earlier. A dozen people had been killed and this young man's only concern was his own safety. The man with the badge walked away from Clint and never looked back. A slow exhale of air was the only outward sign that a problem had been narrowly avoided.

Clint was out of gold coins so it was time to retreat to his cabin, restock and ponder the next move.

Chapter 15

Clint had spent one night under the stars on his way out of Cripple Creek. The cool night air and starlit sky had a soothing effect on his mind. He had made a cold camp, but a warm blanket and canvas had made the overnight rest stop rather nice. It was late Sunday evening when he made the last turn off the main trail onto the winding side road toward his old mining cabin. The two ambush spots that he had identified and used once were just ahead. It was either the memory of those killings or something he sensed that put immediate alarm into his chest. His heartbeat quickened and cooling sweat on the palms of his hands slowed his pace. It was probably a couple of miles from his present spot to safety in the cabin.

A quick dismount and the horse was turned loose to head for the corral and fresh grain. The slack rein would give a jingle as the horse continued on up the road toward his cabin. Clint hung back a good distance and kept to the shadows from the rising full moon. His choice was mostly luck, plus a feeling. Suddenly, the roar of multiple guns firing just ahead of his position was followed by the wailing of his injured horse. Those sounds would have included his own screams if he had not sent his horse forward.

The moonlight clearly showed four men standing around a dead horse and aiming their rifles on up the trail. Clint's second horse must have survived the slaughter and bolted for his cabin corrals. The Wilson men must have assessed that they had missed the muleskinner and his other mount. The second curve in the trail hid the escaping horse within seconds. Clint was now close enough to hear the argument among the men. They were sure the young man got through their fire line and was headed straight for the old mining cabin. Mr. Wilson and one other guard were up at the cabin. The argument was about what story to relate to Mr. Wilson or whether they should all four head for Cripple Creek. The men were so involved in their discussion about their own future that Clint easily and silently slipped by them and their horses.

A steady pace on foot put Clint at his corral barn before any sound of the four Wilson men reached the cabin. He moved around the corral fence and up the water trough to within a few feet of the cabin porch. The trickling of the spring water out of the cabin into the trough that carried the water to the corral below covered any noise. He inched his way up beside the cabin until a knothole gave a fairly good view into the cabin.

There sat Paul Wilson not 10 feet from Clint. He was eating Clint's food and sitting in his chair. His anger was dangerously close to the surface, but Clint contained himself. The revenge was directed only on the man in front of him and not any unlucky other members of this party. The guard in the house was moving from window to door and then back like a caged animal. Wilson seemed very confident and self-assured as he told the guard to ease up. Those shots were probably the death of the cowardly muleskinner. Wilson had asked his men to bring the young man in alive so the source of his gold coins could be determined. Besides, this same young man had also been in the room when Jordan, his best gun hand, had been killed.

The sound of horses arriving at the corral below stopped the guard at the window. A shout from the four men down with the horses caused Wilson to send the guard down to find out what happened. Clint was trying to decide what to do when a wild idea sprang into his head.

Chapter 16

Four days had passed since Paul Wilson and his men had left Cripple Creek. Clint was at his usual table at the café with hot coffee, a stack of pan-fried potatoes with onions, four thick slices of bacon and three eggs just under his fork. This completely calm setting was interrupted by the local law deputy. Clint found himself facing the third-degree questioning about his whereabouts for the past week. Where did he get all those newly-minted gold coins he had so recklessly lost around town?

In his most innocent voice and expression, he asked the deputy about this rough treatment and interest in his life. The lawman shouted back that Paul Wilson had died in that mining cabin that he supposedly owned. Two old miners that were frequent customers of the café came over to the table. These miners knew Clint from the many café visits and personal poker games with him. It was plain they were coming to his rescue as Clint tried to explain he had not been to his cabin for over a week. The deputy was not buying the alibi, but everyone else in the café was on the young man's side.

Clint was somewhat surprised at the support from the other customers due to his social label as a coward. It was fairly clear that the townsfolk did not care for the lawman and his methods. An innocent question by Clint set the stage for the whole story. Why were Mr. Wilson and his men in his cabin while he was away? Private property was almost a sacred creed among western people. No matter how rich and powerful Mr. Wilson had been, he had no right to go into another man's house without an invitation.

Clint sat with trained surprise all over his face as the story about the late Paul Wilson was presented to him. As the story went, Mr. Wilson and five men went up to the old mining cabin to question the young man. After all, the young muleskinner had been in the back room of the gambling hall when the top gun of the Wilson group was killed. On top of that factor was the heavy losses that this young man had had at the poker tables the previous two weeks. His losses had been paid in fresh Denver Mint gold coins, the very same type that was reported stolen by Ute Indians southeast of Canon City. Over the past couple of weeks, over a dozen men had been killed in this region. Most likely all this robbery and murder was related to that gold cache.

The continuing story had the Wilson men attacked by Indians in and around the old mining cabin. Mr. Wilson was bitten by a rattlesnake in the throat. That venomous bite killed Wilson almost instantly. He never identified the attacker. An Indian leather pouch and a rattlesnake tail rattler piece were found in the cabin beside the dead Wilson. No snake was found, not that the men looked very hard for such a deadly beast. Half a dozen gold coins were found in the Indian leather pouch, which was large enough to have held a large rattlesnake.

It was now Clint's turn to tell his story. The whole café was tuned into his every word. The tale that Clint had rehearsed to himself came out smoothly. The gold coins had been traded for some of his horses and the Indians were willing to exchange a large bag of coins for the animals. These Indians didn't seem to have any idea about the true value of the gold coins. It never occurred to Clint that those coins could have been blood money. He was all alone against a large group of Ute Indians, so he accepted their offer without an argument. A sympathetic shrug of his shoulders to the café audience got their complete acceptance. Only the lawman was not happy – but under the critical gaze of this crowd he retreated without another word.

Clint then turned to the understanding café customers with an invitation. Since the gold coins that had come his way were most likely stolen and not really his, how about him using the remaining coins to buy everyone a couple of rounds at the nearest saloon? The exodus from the café was almost instant. The crowd almost carried Clint to the larger saloon about two blocks away. The numbers grew as the herd of people moved down the boardwalk. It was almost midnight when the stack of gold coins on the bar dwindled away. The lawman would have his hands full tonight dealing with all the drunks. This result did bring a soft, warm feeling deep within Clint. The real satisfaction was that he had gotten Paul Wilson for killing his horses and stealing his gold. His revenge on those three riders that had ridden north after his ambush was now complete. Could he stop now knowing that the real leader was most likely living it up in Durango on his hard-earned money?

His thought went back to the mining cabin and his method of doing Wilson in. All the time Clint had spent in and around that cabin was often watched by some elusive rattlesnakes. The den in some rock outcrop just 50 feet away from the cabin was the home base. The rattlesnakes never bothered Clint. He kept his distance and they had always kept clear of the cabin. A couple of times, Clint had harvested a couple of the biggest ones for a rattlesnake dinner. Beef was a lot better, but the change was welcome sometimes. A long pole with a string noose had been prepared for a safe extraction of the desired reptile. It was with this pole and string that Clint snagged a big rattler for Mr. Wilson's demise. To really make the snake mad, Clint had cut the tail rattlers off. A little scratching on the cabin side wall prompted Paul Wilson to stick his head out the side window. The horror that Wilson discovered, was recognition of a large snake with Clint's face right behind it.

The little extra touches of the Ute pouch, gold coins, and snake rattler were just for effect. The useful large rattlesnake was returned to his den. Revenge was sweet and final.

Chapter 17

Cripple Creek fell further behind Clint as his line of horses wound up the mountain road toward Silverton. He had cleared out of his cabin and was packed down with about half of the railroad gold. The other stash was hidden in his dry mine and cabin, anticipating his return in the future. It was a beautiful setting, and if he never made it back, some other lucky prospector might find gold in that old cabin.

He had finally decided that the mission was not complete until Mel Jackson, the leader of the original gang, had been called to account for his actions. Clint had tried to satisfy himself with the revenge on Paul Wilson, Tom Jordan, and Matt Tilson, but the bad taste was still there. Clint had recovered more gold from Wilson than he had ever lost, so that was not the real answer. It was the cold-hearted murder plan of Mel Jackson on a young gambler that had to be challenged. Clint could still see the deadly stare in Jackson's eyes when the last large poker winnings had been pulled into Clint's huge stack. At the time, Clint had not thought much about the bad attitude of the loser, Mr. Jackson. While reading people was one of Clint's major survival skills, that skill was not evident when he had packed up his Silverton winnings and hit the road down to Durango. It was only his split-second reaction that had saved him, but his horse and all his fortune was lost in the dynamite-induced rock slide.

The old miner's ranch was the only stop before he got to Silverton. He had left some very good horse flesh roaming near that burned-out ranch house. As he approached the outbuildings and corral, it really did look like that of an Indian aftermath. It had been a bad trick on the Army and law enforcement, and it had most likely caused additional hatred toward the local Indians. The whole deception had worked for Clint. He had pulled out of Cripple Creek without anyone looking his way for any of the gold coins he was packing. The revenge thing was blamed on the raiding Ute Indians along with the gold heist.

It took most of the next day to locate all his horses. He had purchased some of the best horses from the previous owner of this ranch. The rancher had taken the money and headed for Santa Fe to join some of his family. The Mel Jackson and Paul Wilson gang had killed the old ranch owner's wife in a cattle stampede and stolen most of his cattle. He had sold out the rest of the cattle to Jackson at a fraction of their value, but he was a defeated man. Clint remembered the poor man and the conversations between him and the Silverton stable owner. The rancher had been very pleased to take Clint's cash for his horses. That transaction allowed the man to catch the stage for Santa Fe and escape some of his sorrows and memories.

There was a string of seven good horses stretched out behind his own mount as the winding trail took him to Silverton. It was slow-going and hard work to keep the horses in tow.

The second night west of the ranch brought him to the trail fork. The southwestern fork headed over the steep saddleback that Clint had come over earlier. The northwestern fork climbed higher into the mountains where new gold and silver mines were being actively worked. The roadway from Silverton to this junction was well-traveled. There were a lot of Indian signs all around this area, as this region was the ancestral hunting grounds for several Indian groups. The mining operations and the flood of eastern white settlers had put a lot of pressure on the Indian way of life in this whole region. Clint felt a tinge of pain for the passing of one culture as another crowded into its space. His study of history told him that this was an unending struggle between peoples. The fair and just did not win often in this historic battle for personal space. The strong and cruel often were the dominant forces that prevailed. Clint's little battle against Mel Jackson and his gang was a small gesture of the value of justice – or maybe an attempt to balance power. This line of thinking did help to justify the deadly paybacks he was dishing out.

Two days of hard riding and working the string of horses put Clint into a deep sleep on the third night. Due to his senses being somewhat dulled, a band of Indians was able to almost encircle him before he became fully alert. His position was well-suited for defense, as this was his custom when selecting a campsite. With a fully loaded repeating rifle at his side, the battle could start at any second. The cocking of his rifle sent the signal to the slowly approaching Indians that this sleeping horse wrangler would not be taken easily.

The sleep was out of his eyes and his brain was fully alert. It took only a few seconds for Clint to spot a half-dozen adult male Indians. There was a long silence with no movement by the Indians or Clint. The morning light was just beginning to erase some of the dark holes. The spyglass slowly identified one Indian after another until Clint spotted the two most likely to be the leaders of this band.

A slow squeeze on the rifle trigger let loose a roar that broke the silence. The slug did just as Clint had planned. It smashed a gourd water jug just beside the senior-looking Indian. A sharp order was yelled out to the other Indians and all went silent again. It seemed like an hour before there was any movement at all. Then, out of the brush beside the senior Indian, a young Indian was sent forward with hands spread open wide... a sign of non-aggression. Some hand signs were made that Clint interpreted as a request for trading. These Indians seemed to want Clint's horses and they had pelts and leather goods to trade.

It took over an hour for the trading to get started, as each side distrusted the other. Once the face-to-face bargaining began, the hostile atmosphere quickly dissipated. Business was business and these Indians were good at trading. It was almost noon before all the haggling was completed. As a defensive action, Clint drove a hard bargain. He did not want to show any sign of weakness nor fear even though he was outnumbered 15 to one. The departure was calm and friendly as the Indians led a string of five horses away. Clint continued on his trip to Silverton and Durango now with only two pack horses in tow. The fancy deerskin bags on those horses were loaded with jewelry, gold nuggets and leather goods that would please a queen. Clint's load of gold coins was safely stowed among the Indian valuables.

It was a lot easier to travel with only two trailing horses. Frequent switching of his mounts helped to eat up the distance to Silverton. It was late evening when Clint approached the main street. It must be payday for the miners, he observed, because the street was crawling with happy men and a few fancy ladies. His passage right through Silverton went without notice. It was pure torture to pass so close to those open saloon doors with music flowing out and the sounds of gambling and laughter. The cold camp on the windy high road to Durango nurtured his revenge hatred to an even higher level. Clint was not sure if this heat within him was more about Mel Jackson sitting in a warm hotel in Durango, his cold camp, or missing some top quality gambling. Whatever the true cause, he was ready to extract some blood.

Chapter 18

Durango was a great town for food, drink and gambling. The mining operations were pouring money into this wide-open western town. Clint had spent many hours here watching the pretty dance hall girls, eating great food and winning lots of money. Although he was never a flashy player, his winning streaks did make his face known to a good number of poker players. His target on this visit knew him very well.

Mel Jackson was a rich, flamboyant, arrogant gambler. His bodyguard, Luke Tilson, was feared by most people in these parts. As far as Clint knew, Mr. Jackson had not killed anyone personally, but had others do his dirty work.

A night over at a wagon station just north of Durango had given Clint another note of caution. Luke Tilson was a brother to the Matt Tilson that had disappeared outside of Silverton a few months ago. It was widely known that Luke was on the prowl for anyone that may have been involved in his brother's disappearance.

The third man on Jackson's crew that had ridden south after the rock slide was still unknown to Clint. It would take some undercover work to reveal the identity of that rider. It would not be easy because Mel Jackson knew Clint by sight due to their heated poker games. The only advantage Clint had was that Jackson would think he had killed this young gambler and his horse, and had taken his entire fortune.

Patience was the caution Clint kept telling himself. "Stay out of sight until the third man is identified." He knew that learning the scope of Mel Jackson's operation would be very useful. A direct frontal attack against Jackson personally would not go well with the local law or the businesses that benefited from his activities. His wary self-counsel led Clint to a small livery stable with rooms that were off the main drag. This was the same type of setup Clint had used to his advantage in Silverton. Only the down-and-out miners and ranch hands would do such work as treating horses and cleaning out stables. The livery stable operator was more than eager to have a healthy, young male take his job for a cot off the tack room. Clint could keep his horses in the corral as long as the space wasn't needed. The stable was in bad condition and a little too far from the main part of Durango for heavy demand. It only took a couple of days for Clint to prove his value with horses and physical work. The stable operator soon left Clint to do his work without supervision. The operator was lazy, way overweight, and loved his beer and gossip.

In less than a week, Clint had pieced together enough gossip to paint a fairly good picture of the Mel Jackson operation. The third man that Clint was looking for had to be Jackson's businessman and legal advisor. He went by the name of Gordon Alexander, an overbearing bully on the fat side. He operated out of an office just off of the main street. He was known to be a poor gambler and a womanizer, and also as being extremely shrewd. Jackson himself did not go anywhere for business where Mr. Alexander was not close to his elbow. The rumors had it that Jackson regularly bailed out his legal advisor's gambling debts. It was also part of the gossip that Jackson had intervened on several female complaints of battery against Alexander. Most of these cases had been settled by cash payments to the ladies and free stagecoach tickets out of town.

Clint deprived himself of any purely fun poker games as he tried to put together a plan. The scheme had to target all three of the men that had ambushed him. Luke Tilson was the fast gun of the three – he had killed a half-dozen men in Durango alone. All six killings had been judged fair without any penalty against the gunman. Jackson's lawyer, Mr. Alexander, had played a big part in getting all these shootings declared as self-defense. Tilson's death would not upset anyone in Durango except the Jackson group. Tilson would be Clint's first target.

Keeping out of sight while also tracking Luke Tilson was difficult. It took almost two weeks of hard work to establish the man's pattern of movement. One regular trip by Tilson intrigued Clint: Two or three times per week, just before sunset, he and Alexander would ride due west out of Durango, then return about three or four hours later in the dark. They would head directly for the Golden Nugget Casino and join Mel Jackson until about 2 a.m. Jackson and Alexander would then leave the casino together for the Grand Hotel where they both usually stayed. This pattern was consistent Tuesdays and Saturdays. Sunday night and Monday appeared to be solitary days for all three men.

Clint would finish his work at the stable each day about 4 p.m., and then ride off on his own. This pattern did not raise any questions from the boss. His late return was then done very quietly so as not to give the boss any sense of his going and coming.

It took a couple of weeks for Clint to find the late evening destination of Tilson and Alexander. The fancy complex was well guarded and fortified. The spyglass could not pick up many signs about this operation from Clint's safe distance at night. A weekday trip during daylight was needed for better surveillance.

As a regular gift to himself, Clint went to one of the Oriental bathhouses at least once each week. The hot, soapy water, clean clothes and a glass of top quality wine made for a wonderful break from his mission. This small Chinese bathhouse was just outside the main business area, so it was easy to come and go without drawing any attention to himself. Clint had felt completely anonymous until he started noticing some curious looks from one of the bathhouse attendants. It was a little annoying and surprising because the custom of the Chinese employees was to stay completely out of the way. They normally showed no interest in any individual except to serve and be very polite. The severe glances Clint would catch were definitely out of the ordinary. He knew he had a good physique even if he was rather tan due to his Spanish skin color. The only blemishes were scars from his California battles.

During his fourth trip to the bathhouse, a note was slipped into his freshly cleaned and pressed clothes. Clint was taken by complete surprise to read this perfectly lettered Old English script-style note, "There is a just job for the Bronze Warrior in Durango – Please Help." A flood of fear washed over Clint as he tensed. His California past had caught up to him, and he realized that death could come his way around any corner. He quickly dressed and moved cautiously toward the front desk to pay his bill. A beautiful Chinese woman dressed in the traditional silk gown asked him to follow her to the tea room. Clint felt like bolting for the door for a quick escape. Instead, he held his composure and followed the dainty woman into another room.

The first room was a lavish sitting area, and he was then led through some curtains to an elegant tea room. Three elderly men and two women of similar age were seated around a fairly large octagon table with excellent woodwork. Two very young ladies in fancy dress directed Clint to one of the chairs at the table. Wine and tea selections were offered along with several snack items. Clint could just feel the visual examination he was getting. All the smiles and head bowing were in the friendliest manner, but unnerving nonetheless. Clint selected a red wine and sat sipping the drink waiting for them to act or speak. His nerves were on edge, but his outward appearance was completely calm. He had learned from his Chinese friends in California to just sit quietly and wait.

As if the sky had opened and a fresh breeze suddenly blew through, the oldest gentleman started to speak in excellent, European-style English. The man apologized for interfering in

Clint's daily schedule, but let him know the need was great. It took almost an hour for the whole story to be laid out. Ho Ming, the elder of the Chinese clan in Durango, was a friend of Clint's close acquaintance Le Chen in California.

Chapter 19

Mel Jackson and Gordon Alexander were running a human trafficking operation. They had a network of agents from San Francisco to Durango that moved young Chinese girls off the West Coast ships to Jackson's mansion outside of town. These young females were bought from Chinese traders directly from Chinese ports. Clint was well aware of these operations from his years on the West Coast.

The elder Chinese spokesman, Ho Ming, finally got around to how and when they had identified Clint as the Bronze Warrior. Their close friend and business contact in California had often written about a man that had saved them from ruthless gangs. The specific description of the man, his skin color, body build, battle scars and age matched completely the man that came to their bathhouses in Durango. Some of the young females of Le Chen's operation in California had been abducted and sent to Durango. If this Bronze Warrior was still alive, he would be the one person that Le Chen could trust to free his young ladies.

Le Chen had sent four of his men that the Bronze Warrior had trained to recover the Chinese maidens. Two had been killed. The other two were staying undercover and tracking the abductors. The two Le Chen men were in Durango and could confirm the identity of the girls and the Bronze Warrior.

A slow arch of the elder Chinese man's arm brought two Mexican-dressed Oriental men through the curtains. The mutual recognition was quick and open. A series of bows and smiles cleared the air of any suspicion. Clint knew the two men that had been his students. The two warrior-looking Chinese men were equally pleased to see their teacher and comrade.

The hour was late when Clint finally excused himself. The task ahead was dangerous both for the young ladies they were trying to rescue as well as themselves. Two of these highly skilled Chinese warriors had already been killed. Jackson's fortified holding ranch outside of Durango was well guarded. A plan must be devised that would release the young ladies without harm, but allow Clint to get his three men – Jackson, Alexander and Tilson.

After two days of wrestling with the problem, Clint was no closer to a plan of action. Early the third day, a young Chinese boy slipped Clint a note while he was cleaning up the stables. The message suggested a new insight to the rescue mission. The elderly Chinese man, Ho Ming, at the bathhouse was requesting a meeting.

It was just after dark when Clint finished his stable duties. Durango seemed busier than usual as an overflow of horses needed to be stabled at Clint's workplace. These horse stalls were several blocks off the main street so not many visitors used them on a regular basis. The Chinese bathhouse and laundry was in full swing when Clint slipped in the side entrance. One of the beautiful Chinese young ladies led Clint into the private tea room.

After a short friendly greeting, Ho Ming got to his suggested plan. The businessman and part-time lawyer, Gordon Alexander, had caused his young ladies much anguish over the past couple of years. Alexander was an overweight, sloppy, arrogant bully that constantly harassed the young Chinese ladies. He had beaten several of them when they refused his advances. Mel Jackson had always settled any abuse claims with cash payment to the Chinese head man. Each time Mel Jackson would promise that he would convince Mr. Alexander to leave the young Chinese girls alone. It was well understood by everyone that Ho Ming's young ladies were off-limits. These young, beautiful maidens were here to serve food and drinks and run the bathhouses, stores, and laundries. These ladies would be given in marriage to Chinese men whose large dowries met approval. This was the same arrangement that Clint had seen in Le Chen's vast California operation.

The plan that Ho Ming had devised could work, but had a lot of risks. The part of the plan that would be Clint's was the handling of Mel Jackson's top gun, Luke Tilson. The Chinese men were no match for the ruthless and fast gun hand. Tilson had killed many men and would shoot first then ask questions later. There was one such shooting for which Ho Ming wanted retribution. One of his young ladies had been serving drinks at the Golden Nugget Casino. A visiting gambler raised a question about cheating during a poker game with Alexander and Tilson. The gambler grabbed the Chinese maid as a human shield. Tilson, without hesitation, had shot two bullets right through the midsection of the barmaid. The young Chinese girl and the gambler were both killed. Tilson had gotten off with a claim of self-defense. The Chinese girl's death was written off as an accident and no charges were ever presented. Cheating in poker games was a regular thing for Gordon Alexander. Most people did not challenge him, especially if Luke Tilson was in the game or somewhere nearby. Most locals just avoided Alexander's poker table.

Ho Ming was an elderly statesman with many years of running his business in and around Durango and Silverton. His reputation for running clean bathhouses and laundries was widely respected. His many young Chinese girls and ladies were known for their beauty, manners and clean living. His girls were not part of the female entertainers. Most of these local western men knew and respected Ming's people. An occasional visitor might cause some problems, but these incidents were handled quickly behind the scenes. The primary offender was the overbearing and arrogant Gordon Alexander. It was Alexander's interest in the young beautiful Oriental girls that Ming would use to set a trap.

Clint had his mission when the meeting with Ho Ming was finished. It would be Clint's job to neutralize Luke Tilson. Ho Ming had suggested that a good solid alibi could be provided if and when the need arose. The Chinese people would take care of Mr. Alexander and, hopefully, Mel Jackson at the appropriate time. Ho Ming assured the Bronze Warrior that he would be more than satisfied with the method of dealing justice to Alexander and Jackson. The Chinese master had asked Clint to give him two weeks to set his trap.

Chapter 20

The two weeks that Ho Ming had asked for passed very slowly. Clint had given up his stable job after a nice clean room in one of Ming's boarding houses had been presented to him. The two weeks had allowed some time for poker in an out-of-the-way saloon. These games of chance helped Clint pass the time even though it was at some risk. His face was fairly well known amongst gamblers, so it would be only a matter of time before he was recognized. The rumor was around town that the handsome gambler with lots of money had also been killed a few months earlier.

Clint's surveillance of Mel Jackson and his crew had given him facial recognition of at least a dozen of Jackson's gang. It was near the end of the second week when two of Jackson's men passed through the saloon where Clint was playing poker. Their manners and body language told their mission. They were there to confirm a rumor about the supposedly dead young gambler. The two men tried to be casual, but Clint spotted their arrival and departure. As soon as the two men left the saloon, Clint slipped out the back door into a pitch black alley. He had studied the various escape routes carefully. With his keen memory, moving down the dark alley rapidly was no problem. The real problem would be a planned ambush, but apparently Tilson and Jackson were still investigating rumors. It would be hard for Tilson or Jackson to admit they had missed in an attempted assassination of this skilled young gambler. The dynamite had blown out a huge chunk of the mountain roadway. The resulting rockslide had supposedly carried the rider and horse a good 500 feet down the mountain side. His men had climbed down the rock face and recovered the saddlebags and gold from his dead horse. One of his men had even found the gambler's hat. Tilson himself had a double barrel Dillinger in his vest pocket that the gambler had in his saddlebags. The ivory handles were inlaid with pearl and Chinese symbols. It was a beautiful firearm that no man would give up.

Clint had climbed up the back alley building to a perch on the roof that overlooked several streets. It was less than 30 minutes before Tilson and at least six additional men moved in to surround the saloon. Tilson held his position under a porch across the street from the saloon. Four of his men entered the saloon – two through the back door and two through the front batwings. Clint was close enough to hear some noise from within the saloon. It sounded like chairs and tables being smashed as the men searched the saloon. After things went quite inside the saloon, Tilson's men came out signaling that no one was found. Tilson reappeared from under the porch roof cover and stomped off down the street. His men followed at a very safe distance. They knew the deadly temper of the top gun hand, Tilson.

Now that his cover as a dead man was blown, it was time for action. The next couple of days and nights Clint spent his time tracking Luke

Tilson. The gunman liked his poker games at two favorite gambling halls. Ho Ming provided the bar girls and waitresses on one of these two, the Golden Nugget Casino, the same place where Tilson had killed Ming's young lady. It was now time to coordinate his plan with Ho Ming.

As if their schedules were mystically synchronized, a note was on Clint's bunk requesting a meeting when he got back to his room. Clint had a weird feeling that the old Chinese leader could read his mind. The plan was to entice Alexander out of the casino with a beautiful lady. Clint would advance to the poker table and confront Tilson with an offer for a game of chance between them. Hopefully, the shock of being face-to-face with the man that Tilson thought he had killed would favor Clint. Clint had considerable confidence in his gun skills, but he knew Tilson was extremely dangerous. An unplanned event or random thing often upset the most detailed plan regardless of the skill of the planner. As an extra safety measure, one of the Chinese warriors would have a good view of the selected poker table. Tilson had a habit of occupying the same table and chair as if it was a good luck thing. There was more to that arrangement than anyone knew. Ho Ming's casino maids had reported that some of Mel Jackson's men always rented that particular room each night that Alexander and Tilson played cards down below. This item would have to be addressed.

Clint was having tea with the Chinese leader when the most beautiful lady of all passed through the tea room. She smiled and flirted with Clint, then disappeared through the beaded screen. The older Chinese man smiled as he watched Clint's response to the young lady. Then he asked, "Do you think Gordon Alexander will follow such a woman away from a poker game?" The question did not need an answer.

Thursday night was selected as being most advantageous. Alexander and Tilson usually came to the Golden Nugget Casino on Thursdays, but not always. There was another regular place for Thursday night dinner for Alexander, the King Café. So, an extra enticement would be presented to increase the odds that Alexander would willingly walk into their trap. The beautiful young Oriental lady would parade past the King Café on her way to the Golden Nugget Casino.

All of the Chinese waiters, bar maids, floor sweepers and dishwashers were in top form Thursday night. Alexander was traced from the time he left his hotel room through dinner at the King Café and his trailing of the Chinese maiden to the casino.

Luke Tilson had preceded Alexander to their favorite poker table. Acting as bait, the Chinese maiden had moved on through the casino and was out of sight when Alexander entered the gaming table area. He settled into his regular chair, but was constantly looking around. At least two hours of gambling and drinking passed before the beautiful young woman moved past Alexander's table. Clint watched from a side alcove of the casino. Alexander's eyes never left the young lady's body as she passed ever so close to his table. Their eyes met and Alexander was reeled in like a fish. He left through the side door just a few steps behind the tantalizing woman. He did not return, so Clint moved into the void.

Clint seated himself directly opposite Luke Tilson without an invitation. Their eyes met in instant recognition. Luke was looking into the face of the young gambler that had cleaned him out in Silverton, not three months ago. It was the same face that he was sure he had killed with a load of dynamite up on the rocky mountain road cliffs south of Silverton. The quiver of his hands in rage loosened the pearl-handled Dillinger from his sleeve. He was grasping for the small gun when the first of two bullets slammed into his chest and then his forehead. The gun fight was over almost before it started.

Two young Chinese men in Mexican-style clothes left an upstairs casino room. This was a detail that only Clint observed with a sign of relief. A real party broke out in the casino as the feared gunman's body was hauled from the gaming room. People were gathered around the young gambler telling him how lucky he was to be alive. The local sheriff was getting an earful from a dozen onlookers confirming that Luke Tilson had drawn a sleeve Dillinger on the young gambler that had just taken a seat at the table. It was a pure case of self-defense and the whole crowd would testify to the fact.

The sheriff recommended that the young gambler gather up his belongings and get out of town. Mel Jackson ran a big operation around these parts and the law might not be able to protect the man that killed the organization's top gun. If Jackson's men didn't come gunning for the young man, there would be many seeking the reputation to outdraw the killer of Luke Tilson.

It was early the next morning when Clint left Ho Ming's fancy breakfast feast and headed southeast. He had a load of gold, three fine horses and a feeling that his revenge mission had almost been completed. New Mexico Territory seemed like the right place for his travels. His brother lived down south of Santa Fe. Clint rekindled the old dream of sharing his wealth of gold with his brother.

His revenge had been carried out with two exceptions – Mel Jackson and Gordon Alexander. Ho Ming had assured the Golden Warrior that his method of dealing with these two rascals would be far more painful than a quick death from one of Clint's pistols. A smile came over his face as the green grassland spread out in front of his trail. Very soon he was crossing over the ridge separating the waters of the Rio Grande and the Colorado rivers.

The End

Epilogue

The Durango Messenger newspaper carried the shocking tale of Melborn Jackson's human trafficking operation, and his death. The enslavement of young girls and women for prostitution had been operated out of the rich and flamboyant Jackson's mansion and ranch west of Durango. Gordon Alexander, the man's business manager and lawyer, had protected the operation while taking advantage of the captive girls himself. In graphic detail, the story told how both men's bodies had been discovered near the Mesa Verde cliff dwellings: Each was staked out over an anthill, castrated and tortured with numerous skin cuts. According to the grisly account, many of the cuts appeared to be fingernail scratches.

Jackson's entire ranch had been deeded over to the Chinese businessman Ho Ming, who had vowed to house and rehabilitate the two dozen young women rescued. It was reported that another Chinese businessman and trader from California had arrived in Durango to be reunited with three of his young relatives who had been kidnapped by Jackson's network.

Over a dozen arrests had been made of workers in the human trafficking nightmare. The investigation into who killed Jackson and Alexander was set to continue, despite there being no leads at press time.

About the Author

William F. Martin was born on a Kentucky farm and moved West in the midsixties on an assignment with the federal government's program to help Native Americans. His assignment to Santa Fe, New Mexico, began a lifetime love affair with the American West. His writing interest was developed with the publishing of many technical journal articles and textbooks on environmental and engineering issues. He obtained a BS degree in civil engineering from the University of Kentucky and a MS degree in environmental engineering from the University of Texas.

After assignments in South Dakota, Arizona, and Texas, he has lived near the Gulf of Mexico on Treasure Island, Florida, and in the Blue Ridge Mountains in Boone, North Carolina.